PARTING WORDS

A great murder mystery from Scotland

TRAUDE AILINGER

Published by The Book Folks

London, 2025

ISBN 978-1-80462-309-1

www.thebookfolks.com

PARTING WORDS is the seventh book in a series of amateur sleuth mystery titles set in Edinburgh. For details about the other books in the series, head to the back of this one.

Prologue

He stared at the TV. It couldn't be! Keeping one eye on the news report, he fumbled for the remote. It almost slipped from his trembling fingers, but eventually he managed to hit the pause button. A face filled the screen; angry, defiant. And yet, it was her. A massive adrenaline rush jolted him upright from his prone position on the sofa as if a dead man had been resurrected.

He'd lost track of her, but he'd never stopped looking for her, never stopped thinking about her. How she just upped and left. Not a word, no forwarding address – zilch. How could she? After everything he'd done for her. Who had plucked her from the gutter when she was all alone in the world and without a future? Who had given her a place to stay, given her everything? But she had simply disappeared. Two hundred and eighty-four days ago. And, suddenly, out of nowhere, here she was!

What the hell was she doing, marching alongside long-haired anarchists blocking the ring road? Unbelievable. Why did she always listen to others who put stupid ideas into her head? Maybe it was them who persuaded her to run away, to hide – from him! She would never have left him of her own accord. But now he'd found her, he could make her see how wrong she'd been. He fell to his knees in front of the TV and followed the contours of her face with his fingertips.

"You're mine," he whispered. "And always will be."

Chapter 1

"I don't know!" Martin Eden, subeditor of Forth Write magazine, anxiously flapped his long, thin arms. "It could be dangerous!"

"Don't be silly," his colleague Amy Thornton scoffed. "I'm going undercover in an environmental group, not an organised crime syndicate. They don't know I'm a journalist with close ties to Edinburgh CID. To them I'll just be Simone, a student who wants to do her bit for the environment. And while I'm saving the planet, I'll have a wee nosey around."

Martin flapped some more. "I don't like it!"

"You need somebody on the inside to figure out what is going on," Amy said, "and I'm good at getting men to talk, especially when I do my pretty airhead routine. My only worry is that these guys can't make a decent latte. I bet they only drink herbal tea." She wrinkled her nose. "When I think about it, that sacrifice alone entitles me to be named in the by-line when you reveal the latest corruption scandal in Edinburgh."

Martin raised his arms in horror. "I can't reveal your name; imagine what John would say if–"

He broke off when John Campbell, owner of the magazine, suddenly appeared in the doorway.

A distinguished-looking gentleman in his fifties, he had shunned the role of heir-in-waiting at his mother's shooting estate in favour of being his own boss at the small magazine in Edinburgh's upmarket New Town. *Forth*

Write was not merely a job to him, it was where he felt at home. Martin was his closest friend from their university days, and Amy had become his surrogate daughter after he had fallen head-over-heels in love with her mother.

Generous to a fault and normally imperturbable, he gave his two employees free rein unless Amy was off on one of her crime-busting missions. Her mother Valerie held John personally responsible for her precious daughter's safety and gave him hell if Amy ended up in a dangerous situation, which she frequently did.

"Did I hear my name being mentioned?" he said, with a smile suffusing his plummy accent. "Martin, you are less adept at dissembling than our Amy. Tell me, what are you two up to now?"

Martin sighed. "It's about that huge solar farm out at Currie. Something's amiss."

John pulled up a chair and sat down. "Are you still on that story? I remember there were the usual objections from the local community, but then the guy who was behind it… what was his name again?"

"Jordan Lambie."

"Yes, him. He got planning permission in the end, didn't he?"

Martin nodded. "He did, but I had a feeling there was more to come because the members of The Green Fist won't take this lying down."

"That's this environmental group, isn't it?" John asked. "Why would they be against solar power?"

"They believe all technology is inherently evil," Martin said. "Anyway, last week I went back to Currie to get reactions to the final decision."

"I don't see why you bothered," said John, "unless the locals resort to crime to stop the project."

"So far, they haven't, although there was a lot of banner-waving and noise at the local library. No, I think it is Jordan Lambie who has bent the rules."

John's salt-and-pepper eyebrows rose with sudden interest. "Ah, really?"

"While I was there, I popped into the local butcher's shop. The owner was one of the people whose land was to be used for the development. I said he must be pleased that the matter was finally settled. He seemed embarrassed and said he wasn't selling his land after all. When I asked why, he was very cagey. There were other people in the shop, so I didn't press him. I caught up with him later, but he said he was busy and didn't want to be in the newspapers."

"That's his prerogative," John said, "and so is changing his mind about–"

Martin lifted his hand.

"Yes, but Jordan Lambie won't be quite so reasonable about it. I looked at the map and did a quick calculation of the cost. Without the butcher's land, the whole project becomes unviable, but it still hasn't been called off."

John tilted his head. "What does this Jordan Lambie have to say about all this?"

"He doesn't speak to the press. He is a very private man as well, apparently."

"That's not a crime either," John said mildly. "Sorry, Martin, I'm a bit slow on the uptake. I still don't see a story here."

"Look." Martin spread out a map of the Currie district and pointed to a circled area south of the main road. "This is the only patch of land that could sensibly replace the large field owned by the butcher."

"And who does that belong to?" John asked.

"I had to call in a favour from a guy at the land registry," Martin said. "The owner is a bloke called Donald Murray. His land lies directly on the village boundary and was not included in the original application, and not in the public consultation either. Using his land now would make the whole project illegal. There's a lot of money at stake here."

John stroked his immaculately shaved chin. "Can you find out – legally, I mean – whether this sale has gone through before we print a story that leaves us open to a libel action?"

Martin shrugged. "The council's been stonewalling, citing confidentiality and privacy laws and whatever else they can think of. The other problem is that this Donald Murray is a member of The Green Fist. Why would he sell his land to facilitate a project that his own group is so fiercely fighting against?"

"Ah, I see," John said. "And you think that over a mug of kombucha, and a vegan slice, our Amy could charm Mr Murray into a confession?"

"I'm still here, you know," Amy said irritably. "I think Martin is right, and there is something fishy going on." She looked pleadingly at her boss, knowing fine well that he had never been able to refuse her anything. "Please, John, can I go? If you don't tell Mum, I won't either."

John sighed. "Well, if the project is illegal and someone in the council covered it up, this could be quite an explosive story. At least you're not getting involved in any murder down there, so your mum can't accuse me of recklessly endangering your life. Do we know anything about this fellow Murray?"

"Retired science teacher," Amy said. "He founded The Green Fist thirty-odd years ago, although it was called The Green Fingers then. He lives above the zero-waste shop that doubles up as the group's office. I've phoned them this morning and spoke to a woman called Keira. She said that she would be in this afternoon. Fingers crossed that Murray is there, too. This Keira sounded lovely." She smiled encouragingly at John. "It'll be perfectly safe."

And since this was all he was ever really worried about, Amy got ready to go undercover.

Chapter 2

A few hours later, Amy was on her way to the small village of Currie. Roughly one mile west of the Edinburgh city bypass, it stretches along the north side of Lanark Road. Having expanded in the seventies as an overflow of the ever-growing city, it is the poor cousin of the neighbouring, more affluent villages of Balerno and Juniper Green. To the south, invisible from the road, the Water of Leith flows through a deep, wooded gorge towards the city. Amy drove past fields of horses and forage crops, feeling some sympathy for the residents who resented the prospect of this idyllic scene being spoilt by a sea of shiny, blue-black panels.

In keeping with her new persona, a second-year Modern Languages student at Heriot-Watt University, she had temporarily dispensed with her usual skilfully applied make-up and the unique and stylish clothes her mother had always sewn for her. Instead, she had pulled out from the bottom of her wardrobe the faded jeans, old trainers and baggy T-shirt that she used on such occasions.

Conscious that her mother's vintage MG, a family heirloom, was also inconsistent with her cover, she pulled into a small retail park off the main road and walked the rest of the way.

From reading dozens of spy novels, she knew to stay as close to her real identity as possible to avoid slip-ups that might unmask her. Should anybody involve her in a conversation in French, she was confident that she would be able to hold her own, thanks to her misguided plans of becoming a French teacher after leaving school. Her ignorance in matters of the environment would be an advantage rather than a problem, because in her experience, people were much less guarded in the presence of those they perceived as clueless.

When she arrived at the address given online, her anticipation turned to elation as the smell of freshly ground coffee beans greeted her inside. It was a small shop selling staple foods and cleaning products from refillable cylindrical dispensers.

On the right-hand side of the room stood a couple of tables and chairs in front of a counter displaying a coffee machine with a half-full carafe on the warming plate and a small selection of traybakes, some covered in thick chocolate. On the wall behind it, there were shelves with bags of coffee beans and tea leaves.

Amy was congratulating herself on her choice of assignment, when a man in his early sixties emerged from the next room, frowning and quickly closing the door behind him. As soon as he saw her, his forehead smoothed, and a broad smile replaced an expression of suspicion.

"Good afternoon," he said with an educated Edinburgh accent. "Can I help you?"

Amy had done her homework on the most prominent group members. Corduroy trousers and tweed jacket, an expansive forehead and small, half-moon glasses perched on the tip of a fleshy nose whose mauve hue betrayed the owner's liking for a tipple or two in the evening – this had to be the founder and former leader of The Green Fist, Donald Murray.

"Hi, I'm Simone. Keira told me I could pop in this afternoon. I'd like to become a member of The Green Fist."

"Oh, yes, she mentioned you. The more, the merrier. Welcome!"

He invited her in with a sweeping gesture of his arm that just happened to touch her shoulders. Amy instinctively moved away but quickly plastered a smile on her face. She didn't want to antagonize him during their first meeting. He pulled back with an apologetic smile and a twinkle in his eye as if to say, 'you can't blame me for trying'.

"I'm Donald Murray, and before you ask, no relation of the famous Andy. My friends call me Donnie."

He stretched out both his hands to grasp hers.

"I'm Simone Fleming. No relation of the famous Alexander," she said, pulling away. "Nice to meet you, Donnie. I was hoping I could do something for you, I mean" – Amy hastily corrected herself in case the old goat interpreted this as encouragement – "for the group. I was wondering how I could help. I'd like to do *something* about, you know, climate change and all that, but I'm not sure where to start."

"You've come to the right place, Simone," Murray said, pulling a sheet of paper and a pen out of a drawer behind the counter. "Just fill in this form with your name and contact details. We ask members to pay five pounds a month to help fund any campaigns we run. Is that alright with you?"

"Sure," Amy said, jotting down her undercover name and a fake address. "Can I pay in cash?"

Murray winked. "Of course. No need for Big Brother to know everything about us."

He stuffed the five-pound note into a carved wooden box, countersigned the form and put everything back into the drawer.

"Let me introduce you to Keira. She's been making bird feeders to raise funds. Do come through."

Her hope of a latte and tiffin fading, Amy followed Murray into the adjoining room where a young woman, almost a girl still, was sitting at a long table, holding pieces of wood and wire mesh together. She seemed tense, but visibly relaxed when she saw Amy enter in Murray's wake.

"It's okay," he said soothingly. "Keira, this is Simone, our new recruit."

"Oh, yeah, hi," Keira said. "Grab a seat, Simone. I'm almost done."

She had a pretty doll's face and a shy smile. Her eyes shone as she proudly nodded towards the row of bird feeders on the shelf behind her.

"What do you think we can charge for those?" she asked Amy.

"They look great," Amy said. "At least fifteen pounds, I'd say. Do you sell bird food as well?"

"Ha," Keira said to Murray with some glee, "I told you we should. You've got to make it easy for people. If somebody decides to buy the feeder on a whim but then has to go to another shop to buy the seeds, they might not bother."

Amy nodded. "That's exactly my thought."

Murray shook his head self-mockingly. "I've told you, Keira, you must stand in the election for our next group leader."

Keira gave a little laugh. "Rubbish. Pamela is doing a great job. I could never be like her." She turned to Amy. "Pamela is a force of nature—"

"That's a nice way of putting it," Murray muttered with a bitter undertone that did not escape Amy's notice.

"And she's my best friend. I don't know why you two are always at each other's throat," Kiera said. "Another one finished!" She released her grip on the feeder, and satisfied that it would not fall apart, placed it on the shelf next to the others. "Time for a coffee?"

Amy agreed enthusiastically and followed them back into the shop. Keira had stepped up to the window and was scanning the road outside. Despite the sunlight streaming in, she shivered in her flowery summer dress and wrapped a long cardigan tightly around herself.

"Relax," Murray told her, taking her by the arm and guiding her to one of the tables. "He won't try anything while we're here." He turned to Amy. "Keira's ex turned up out of the blue a couple of months ago," he said by way of an explanation. "A nasty piece of work. If I were a little younger… Coffee or tea, Simone?"

"Coffee, please. Is your ex-boyfriend bothering you?" Amy asked Keira.

Keira said nothing. She cradled the coffee mug Murray had placed on the table for her but shook her head at the tiffin he offered her. With an encouraging nod, he pushed it towards Amy, who happily accepted it.

"He should be in prison," Murray said to Amy with a concerned side glance at Keira, "but the police are not doing anything. Absolute disgrace. He did terrible things to her when Keira lived in Glasgow, and when she broke off with him, he stalked her. Keira fled to Edinburgh, but when he found out, he followed her here."

Murray handed Amy her mug and put a milk jug and a sugar bowl on the table.

"I should never have gone to that demo," Keira whispered. "It was such a stupid thing to do."

Murray banged his fist on the table, making the mugs wobble dangerously. "You should be able to do what you want, love, not have your life ruined by a scumbag like him."

Amy was about to suggest reporting the incident using her contacts in CID but caught herself in time.

"You should go to the police again," she said instead. "Nobody has the right to control your life like this."

Just then, a young man with a long ponytail and dreamy blue eyes entered the shop.

"Ready?" he said to Keira, barely acknowledging Murray and Amy.

"Yes, let's go," Keira said, snatching her bag. "I need to be home by five."

With the young man protectively hovering over her, they left.

"Young Aiden has taken to picking her up and walking her home. That's how frightened she is," Murray told Amy. "Although we all know he has an ulterior motive." He chuckled. "Personally, I think a young woman is better off with a more mature, experienced lover. Don't you think?"

"Is Keira married?" Amy asked, pointedly ignoring his question. "I noticed the ring."

"Yes, she met her husband after she'd moved to Edinburgh about a year ago, and they got married soon afterwards. A bit too soon if you ask me. He's very protective, but I think he doesn't understand what she really needs. If he had his way, she'd stay at home all day to keep safe, but that's not the person she is. I'm not sure he knows how much time she spends here with us, and it's probably better that way. He doesn't like us much, not since Pamela took over the reins, anyway."

"Why? What's he got against the group?" Amy asked, wondering how she could direct the conversation from the interesting but irrelevant topic of Keira's marriage towards the solar panel project.

Murray chuckled again, clearly pleased to be able to impress Amy with his superior knowledge. "Ah, you don't know that Keira's husband is Jordan Lambie."

Amy could not believe her luck.

"Should I?" she asked innocently. "Who is he?"

Murray peered at her over his half-moon glasses. "Jordan Lambie is a major shareholder in NPE, that is Northern Power Energy. He wants to build a big solar farm in this area. You must have read about that in the press. He has invested most of his own money to create a Scottish energy company to compete with the 'big boys' of the industry."

"So, what's his problem with The Green Fist?" Amy asked to keep Murray talking. "We need to come off fossil fuels, so we're all on the same side, aren't we?"

He sighed.

"Pamela, our great leader, has been fighting the project from the start. Wrong decision, in my humble opinion, but I'm out of touch, apparently."

A rattle at the letter box made him jump.

"At last! All day I've been waiting. Royal Mail, pah! Snail mail, more like. You're lucky if you get a letter within a week these days. Even first class takes at least two days. And only yesterday, their chairman got a huge bonus. Ridiculous!"

Murray yanked out the letter stuck in the bristles of the flap in the door and tore it open. He read and reread the contents as a smile spread about his face.

"Good news?" Amy asked.

"Yes." Suddenly reticent, he smoothed the letter almost tenderly. "I must go. Would you excuse me? I need to lock up. I won't hear the bell from my flat upstairs."

"Of course," Amy said and rose hastily. "Thank you for the coffee and the tiffin."

Murray nodded absent-mindedly. Absorbed by the news, he had completely forgotten that Amy had ostensibly come to help out.

Amy turned to go but not before she had caught a glimpse of the letterhead. Spire Healthcare. A retired science teacher going private?

As the door clunked shut behind her and the key turned in the lock, she tried to make sense of what she had seen and heard. Judging by the butterflies in her stomach, she was onto something. What exactly, however, she was not sure… yet.

* * *

Amy and Martin had spent several days sitting at their desks in the spacious office of *Forth Write* magazine in

George Street looking for background information on the people involved in the solar panel project. For all his eccentric demeanour, Martin Eden was a shrewd operator and had forgotten more about the goings-on in Edinburgh than most other journalists would ever know.

He had badgered an old school friend who worked for the council to keep his eyes and ears open for any gossip about the project, while Amy had built a picture of the lives and loves of Donald Murray. The breakthrough came just as the late summer sun pierced the thick blanket of clouds and bathed the severe, grey Georgian buildings across the road in a golden light.

"I think, I've got it!" Amy exclaimed. "I've spent ages looking for any indication why Murray might enlist the services of a private healthcare clinic, and I couldn't find anything. He is a Munro bagger, so there can't be too much wrong with him."

"Maybe not physically," Martin said, "but why would you make it your life's ambition to clamber up two hundred and eighty-two Scottish mountains? Gale-force winds! Horizontal rain!" He shuddered at the thought. "He must have some underlying mental health issues."

"Only because you had one bad experience going up Ben Nevis–"

"Bad experience?" Martin screeched indignantly, flapping the long, wide sleeves of his ethnic-print smock in distress. "I was traumatized! Three hours I dragged myself up there, step by arduous step, and what did I see at the top? Nothing! A wall of impenetrable fog, a–"

"Do you actually want to hear what I've found out or not?" Amy asked with a hint of irritation in her voice.

"Of course I do, my darling, sorry," he said, wiping his forehead theatrically as if trying to erase the painful memory of his one and only hike in the Scottish hills.

"I went deeper into his contacts on social media, and guess what? Murray has a daughter who is ill. Cancer. The waiting lists are shocking, so I think they're going private.

Spiral Healthcare offer cancer treatments, but they don't come cheap. So, where would a retired teacher get that kind of money from?"

"The sale of land to a developer!"

Martin gave Amy a hug that almost drowned her in colourful cloth and planted a kiss on her forehead.

"You're a genius," he said. "Murray must have sold his patch of land to Lambie to save his daughter."

"And he doesn't like the politics of the new leader of The Green Fist anyway," Amy mumbled, a fold of fabric in her mouth. "She is far more radical than Murray ever was."

She wriggled free from Martin's embrace and came up for air. "Murray has kept shtum about the sale because he won't want the other members of The Green Fist to find out that he betrayed their cause."

"And Lambie also wants to keep the whole deal under wraps," Martin said, "because the local community would start the whole process of objections again, and this time they would probably succeed because Murray's land goes right up to the village boundary." He grabbed Amy's shoulders. "If we're right, there must have been a few backhanders to members of the council... They should have insisted on a new consultation process, but they've simply waved the project through." Martin threw his arms in the air. "Corruption, right in the centre of local government!"

"Is that project such a bad thing, though?" asked Amy. "I know it's a shame to cover fields with solar panels, but we need more renewable energy, and Murray needs the money to save his daughter's life. It's a win–win situation, isn't it?"

Martin held Amy at arm's length and tutted. "Democracy always takes precedence, my darling. Always. These procedures might be tedious, but we can't have people ignoring regulations and running roughshod over the local community like that."

Amy shook him off. "They're just a bunch of Nimbys. Our electricity has to come from somewhere. Don't you think it's much more of an issue that a woman like Keira Lambie doesn't dare walk home alone because she is being stalked? *That's* a scandal!"

"You're right, of course," Martin said. "But that's your domain, not mine. Why don't you do a feature on stalking?"

Amy sat up. "That's exactly what I'm going to do. We need to get those bastards off our streets."

Martin looked suddenly worried. "Listen, darling, don't you get involved with those people. Concentrate only on the victims, do you hear?"

But Amy had already started up her computer.

Chapter 3

Some days later, Detective Inspector Russell McCord was dealing with a major crisis. And not particularly successfully, it had to be said. With a soundtrack of groans, interspersed with muttered obscenities, he was typing furiously for a few seconds, then stabbing the delete button as if it had personally offended him, only for his fingers to start attacking the keyboard again.

"Are you okay, sir? Can I help at all?" Detective Sergeant Duncan Calderwood asked, gently placing an americano and a lemon muffin in front of his boss.

Normally this did the trick in times of stress, but McCord only glanced regretfully at the proffered refreshments as if they belonged to a previous, more carefree life.

"You're a good man, Calderwood," McCord said with feeling, "but I need to do this on my own."

"No, you don't," Calderwood said and pulled up a chair. "That's what friends are for."

McCord's fingers slowed and came to rest on the keyboard, covering the page with a cascade of meaningless letters. His chest had suddenly become tight as he realised that Calderwood had never called him 'friend' before. He noisily cleared his throat.

"Do you have any experience in writing a best man's speech? In particular for your father and his bride?"

"I'm afraid not," Calderwood said. "My father, boring bourgeois that he is, has only been married once, and he likes to follow the rule book; although, if my maths is correct, my parents must have been in a bit of a hurry to get hitched. But we could watch *Four Weddings and a Funeral* to see how not to do it."

McCord stared uncomprehendingly at his giggling partner. "Don't be stupid, Calderwood," he said. "How is gatecrashing people's private functions going to help? And my dad is certainly not on the way out yet. I sometimes think he is fitter than me."

Calderwood pulled out his phone to educate his boss in cinematic history but before he could show him the movie poster, McCord shook his head.

"I know, I know, the Internet is full of templates and whatnot, but it needs to be personal. It needs to be… from me."

"Why don't you start with some of your memories?" Calderwood suggested. "How you met Clare for the first time, maybe?"

McCord remembered the maelstrom of anxiety that had enveloped him when his dad had first broken the news that he was dating somebody. It had always been him and his dad from day one when his mother had died giving birth to him, leaving a grief-stricken husband and a baby son behind who to this day could not shake off a feeling of guilt and a need for atonement.

"I was relieved that she wasn't the stereotypical evil stepmother," he said. "I thought she was quite nice, actually, right from the start."

Calderwood heaved a little sigh. "Something like that," he said slowly. "But maybe introduce a touch of humour and try to be a bit more… enthusiastic?"

McCord stared at him. "What do you mean, 'enthusiastic'?"

Calderwood sighed again.

"You're not much help, you know," McCord grumbled.

When the phone rang, McCord grabbed it with the desperation of a drowning man.

"McCord!"

His face lit up as he listened to the voice at the other end, and he smiled as he put the receiver down.

"What is it?" Calderwood asked. "Is the wedding off?"

"Of course not, Calderwood. What's the matter with you? You've been spouting nonsense all evening. My dad and Clare are perfect for each other. No, there's been a suspicious death in Currie. Come on, the speech will have to wait."

* * *

Caulderhame Road was a pleasant cul-de-sac lined with a terrace of modern two-bedroom dwellings boasting a playful portico at each entrance. The small patches of lawn in front had all been liberally treated with weedkiller and mowed to half an inch of their life. Small globes of orange light emanated from the streetlights, illuminating a slight drizzle so gentle that it seemed to caress the skin.

The respectable and peaceful ambience, however, had been spoilt by the arrival of the small army of people required to mop up after a violent death. PC Jim Easton, whose worn-out look and stoic manner betrayed a lifetime in the service, showed McCord and Calderwood into the living room. After coming in from the damp outside, it felt very warm. McCord's eyes were immediately drawn to the dying flames in the wood burner.

"Odd to have a fire going at this time of year," he remarked.

"Still quite mild for the beginning of September," Easton agreed. "I like a real fire myself, but it won't be long until they make those wood burners illegal. And then we'll have nothing in the winter to keep us warm during power cuts. The wife and I have even stocked up on candles; looks like they did as well." He pointed to a row of unused candles lined up on the fireplace.

McCord was not going to be drawn into an evaluation of the Scottish government's environmental policies even though he liked the physical manifestations of death even less than politics. Blood and gore made him queasy, and he was grateful for people like Dr Cyril Crane who inexplicably seemed to enjoy rummaging around in a corpse to find the cause of death.

"Ah, DI McCord, DS Calderwood! Always a delight!" The pathologist briefly paused in packing his bag as McCord cautiously entered the living room in his overshoes. "Not much of a mystery here, I'm afraid. Blunt force trauma to the skull as a result of a fall. Something more interesting might come up in the PM and the tox report, but there's little doubt about the cause of death."

McCord frowned. "An accident, then?"

"Well, the severity of the impact indicates that she was pushed or ran away from an attacker at some speed. She fell backwards and hit her head on the edge of the coffee table." Crane thoughtfully pointed out the large bloodstain in case the detectives had missed it. "Sadly, our skulls are not designed for that sort of treatment."

"Would she have died instantly?" McCord asked.

"Not necessarily," Crane said, "but there was little chance she could have survived a head trauma like this."

The SOCO who had been taking close-up pictures of the wound indicated that he was done and proceeded to document the sections of floor around the body.

McCord kept out of his way but could not delay looking at the victim any longer. A very young woman, dressed in a short, polka-dot dress, lay on the floor. One of her fluffy slippers had come off, revealing a small, unevenly tanned foot. Draped around a face that looked almost childlike in death, was long, shiny chestnut hair that covered most of the wound as if to spare McCord the sight.

"Mrs Keira Lambie," Easton explained. "Husband called it in."

"Where is he now?" McCord asked.

When faced with any violent death, McCord always suspected the close relatives first. In his experience, the family was not always the haven it should be.

"PC Reid took him to the Riccarton Inn," Easton said.

"What?" McCord exclaimed. "Why?"

Easton remained calm. He was probably used to irate DIs questioning his competence.

"Mr Lambie was in a terrible state, sir. We had to get him out of the house for his own sanity and to let forensics get on with their job. He has no relatives nearby, so he asked to be taken to the Riccarton Inn. It's just a few minutes away, so we took a preliminary statement, and then PC Reid drove him there. Mr Lambie said he was going to take some sleeping pills and would be available tomorrow if we needed to ask him more questions."

"Did he tell you what happened?"

"He said there was an intruder, but he didn't see him. There are signs of a break-in at the back door, if you want to have a look."

Crane put on his raincoat. "I'd like the body to be taken to the morgue as quickly as possible. Human remains don't keep well at room temperature. I take it you have seen enough, DI McCord?" A sardonic smile played around his mouth.

"Quite," McCord replied evenly. "She's all yours."

McCord was relieved to get away from the body and gladly followed Easton through the hall and into the kitchen where another SOCO was dusting the back door for fingerprints. The frame was splintered in places where somebody had forced the door. The floor was covered in muddy footprints.

"Any luck with those?" McCord asked.

"They're from the husband when he ran outside to chase the intruder and came back in," the SOCO said. "He pretty much covered the whole floor with mud. Not much chance of finding anything else on it, I'm afraid."

"How convenient," McCord remarked.

"I asked Mr Lambie to leave his shoes so we could eliminate his prints," Easton said.

McCord nodded appreciatively.

"Good thinking. Has anybody been round the neighbours yet to ask if they saw or heard anything?"

"PC Reid is away doing that right now."

"Excellent. Anything else I need to know?"

"The ambulance driver told me to pass on that the victim tried to tell him something, but she was struggling to speak, and her words didn't make any sense."

"Where is he?"

"He was called out to another emergency. Mrs Lambie was beyond help by then, so he went off. But he wrote it all down."

Easton pulled out a piece of paper and gave it to McCord. "He asked her if she knew who had done this to her, and that's all he could make out."

"'Aye... but... proven... pa... mella,'" McCord read aloud. "Would she not have tried to tell us the name of her attacker?"

He read the note again. "Could the last bit be 'Pamela'? Any idea who that might be?"

Easton shook his head.

There were footsteps in the hallway, and PC Douglas Reid appeared in the door frame. After introductions had been made, he gave McCord the bad news.

"It seems all the neighbours had drawn their curtains and were watching telly, so nobody noticed anything unusual around the time of death."

McCord turned to Calderwood. "Great. Looks like we have absolutely nothing to go on apart from an uncertain reference to a Pamela."

"I got something interesting from two of the neighbours, though," Reid said.

McCord swivelled back to face the PC. "Go on?"

"Both noticed a man hanging around the street on several occasions in the past couple of weeks, and he was here this afternoon as well."

McCord perked up. "Description?"

"A bit vague," Reid said. "Young, average height, always wearing a green hoodie. When one of the neighbours approached him before, he immediately ran off. They remembered some of the dates and times. I'll write up my notes and send the report over asap."

"Thanks."

With a nod, Reid left the room.

"It's not much to go on, is it," McCord said with a sigh.

"At least the husband was telling the truth about an intruder," Calderwood replied. "Shouldn't be long until we've got the case wrapped up."

McCord watched the covered remains of Keira Lambie being carried out to the hearse. "Let's hope so."

* * *

While McCord and Calderwood were making their way to St Leonard's police station to set up the investigation, John Campbell was carrying a bottle of champagne through to the living room in his elegant flat above the premises of *Forth Write* magazine. He expertly uncorked it, filled four glasses and lifted his to toast his old friend.

"Tonight, all the readers of *Forth Write* magazine can sleep peacefully in the knowledge that any illegal dealings will be uncovered and exposed by Edinburgh's most esteemed instrument of justice, and that the green fields of Currie will remain unspoilt. Here's to Martin and his latest scoop!"

"To Martin," Amy and her mother Valerie echoed, but Amy's lips had hardly touched the bubbly liquid when her phone buzzed.

Valerie shot her a disapproving look.

"I need to know what's going on in the city," Amy said defensively. "It could be…" She stopped herself.

"A murder, exactly," Valerie finished the sentence for her, glowering.

"Don't start, Mum, please," Amy said. "I'm–"

"Salmon oatcakes, anyone?"

But John's attempt to deflect yet another squabble between mother and daughter failed as Amy excitedly scrolled down her screen.

"Something's happened in Currie," she said. "Police, ambulance, forensics van, oh, and a hearse. Caulderhame Road. Ring any bells, Martin?"

"That's where Jordan Lambie lives! I tried to doorstep him once, but he wasn't at home." He put down his glass, suddenly looking worried. "I hope he hasn't killed himself because of my article! That would be awful!"

"It's much more likely that one of the residents has bumped him off," Amy said. "Wouldn't it be ironic if he was killed on the day the solar panel project was going down the pan anyway?"

"That would be such a relief," Martin said.

"To know that somebody's been murdered?" Valerie asked, outraged. "Am I the only one here who has any moral parameters?"

"There's an easy way to find out," Amy said, ignoring her mother's outburst. "After all, I do know somebody in the force."

Martin clapped his hands excitedly. "Oh, goodie, do give DI McCord a call!"

Amy didn't need telling twice; she had already hit the speed dial button.

Valerie glared at Martin. "Stop encouraging her," she reprimanded him, but he stoically took the hit. He had been scheming for what seemed an age to pair off Amy and DI McCord, but so far, they had stubbornly refused to get romantically involved.

"What's going on in Currie?" Amy asked without preamble when McCord picked up.

There was a pause at the other end. McCord was always surprised how fast news travelled through the ether via mobile phone masts and satellites, although he should know by now.

"Suspicious death," he said. "Looks like an intruder got into the house."

"Who's the victim?" Amy asked. "Jordan Lambie?"

"No, his wife, Keira," McCord said. "How–"

"Keira? Oh, no!"

Amy pictured Keira in the pretty summer dress she had been wearing and remembered her joy at the bird boxes she had made. And she also remembered her fear.

"You knew her?" McCord asked. "Why does that not surprise me? Have you heard of a Pamela in connection with her?"

"As a matter of fact, I have. A Pamela Boyd is the leader of the local eco group, The Green Fist. Why?"

"Keira Lambie tried to tell the ambulance driver something. Most of it was unintelligible, but the end of it could have been 'Pamela'."

"I don't think she meant that Pamela was her killer. They were close friends," Amy said. "I had the impression that Pamela Boyd was a kind of mentor to Keira."

"Still, it's her the victim mentioned, so we need to find her asap. At least now we have her surname, so that should be easy."

"You're barking up the wrong tree," Amy said. "It's not Pamela you should be looking for."

"Please don't tell me you have a theory already."

"I have more than that," Amy said. "Keira Lambie was being stalked by her former boyfriend. He should be in prison, but the police did nothing, as usual."

"And where did you get this nugget of information?" McCord asked.

"From a guy called Donald Murray. He's a member of The Green Fist, where I met Keira only last week."

McCord needed a moment to process this.

"When did you become a tree hugger?"

"I went undercover," Amy said, with no small amount of pride. "In fact, I'm with Mum and John celebrating Martin's scoop. He wrote our main feature this weekend exposing how Keira's husband bypassed all regulations to push through a very unpopular project in the Currie area."

Amy heard McCord scribbling notes on a piece of paper.

"Hm. Maybe this case is a little more complicated than I thought."

"No, it's not," Amy said. "Find the ex-boyfriend. Keira was so scared of him that she got another member of the group to walk her home."

"Do you have the name of the ex-boyfriend, by any chance?"

"Not yet," she admitted. "I'll get onto it."

"Good. But if you find him, stay away from the guy. We'll deal with him. Understood?"

"Yes, sir; of course, sir," Amy said mockingly, and hung up.

She turned triumphantly to her mother.

"See? Edinburgh CID needs me. They didn't have a clue about the stalker. And McCord has expressly forbidden me to go near him; he always lectures me on safety although it is patronising and entirely unnecessary. So, Mum, you can relax and enjoy the evening."

"Well, cheers to that," John said, raising his glass again. "Let's get this miracle of viniculture down our throats before it goes completely flat."

Chapter 4

Hearing Amy's voice on the phone had reminded McCord of the double dilemma his dad had landed him with. Not only was he to write a speech, but he was also to bring Amy to the wedding at Dalhousie Castle as his plus-one.

To his surprise, she had readily agreed when he had finally plucked up the courage to ask her, but so far none of their outings together had ended in anything but disaster. And now he was not only in danger of messing up with Amy – again – but also ruining his dad's big day with a dreadful speech. Or, worse, no speech at all. The case. He needed to concentrate on the case.

"Have you got an address for this Pamela Boyd yet?" he asked Calderwood.

"Yes, 110 Lanark Road West, just a few minutes from here."

"Well, let's hope she has mud on her shoes and a bloodied top in the laundry basket."

* * *

Pamela Boyd lived in a modest semi with a front garden that had been thoroughly rewilded. It occurred to

McCord that he could persuade the other owners of his shared back lawn to do the same; they were not enamoured with him because by the time he got round to mowing it, somebody less tolerant of grass two feet high had beaten him to it. Nobody had ever said anything to him, probably because they feared immediate arrest, but he could tell. He suspected, though, that if he suggested rewilding, his real motive would be a little too transparent.

"It doesn't look as if she's done a runner," Calderwood said, pointing to the bikes in the drive and the light behind the tightly closed curtains.

"Either innocent or brazen," McCord said and rang the bell.

The woman who opened the door was in her fifties and wore a large, grey apron and a baggy T-shirt that had seen better days.

Her short brown hair, streaked with grey, had been cut with no-nonsense precision, and her eyes, fixed on McCord, were sharp and intelligent.

"Yes, can I help you?"

"Detective Inspector McCord, and this is Detective Sergeant Calderwood," McCord said, flipping open his ID. "Ms Pamela Boyd?"

"The very same," she said. "What do you want?"

"We need to speak to you about Mrs Keira Lambie. Do you mind if we come in?"

It was obvious that Pamela Boyd minded very much.

"Keira?" she asked, not budging from the threshold. "Why?"

"I'm the one asking the questions," McCord said, his irritation rising. "And I can ask them at the station as well if you prefer and get a forensics team in here within twenty minutes."

"Forensics?" Boyd asked, but her show of surprise did not convince McCord. "What's happened to Keira?"

"It would be better if we went inside, Ms Boyd," Calderwood said in his conciliatory manner. "We're hoping that you can assist us with our investigation."

"Investigation into what?" she asked but stepped backwards, allowing them to enter the narrow hall. All the doors coming off it were closed.

Calderwood regarded Boyd with a sad smile. "We believe that you are a friend of Mrs Keira Lambie, is that correct?"

"Yes, I am," Boyd said, looking worried now.

"I'm afraid we have bad news."

Boyd turned her back to them and opened the door to a small kitchen and switched the light on. She pointed to the four chairs around a wooden kitchen table.

"Have a seat."

The room smelled faintly of paint, but the faded wallpaper had seen a fair bit of living.

"I'd rather sit somewhere more comfortable," McCord said and, with Calderwood right behind him, made his way back down the hall.

He opened the door to the right, and they found themselves in a good-sized living room. It was covered in newspaper, bedsheets of various sizes and open pots of paint. Three pairs of eyes stared at them suspiciously.

"They're police," Boyd explained, squeezing into the room behind the detectives.

"Are you going to arrest us?" asked an anxious-looking elderly lady with orange paint spatters on her wrinkled face.

"You can't!" a young woman with blue hair squealed.

"Told you, Scotland has become a police state!" declared a young man with a goatee. "We're only exercising our citizen's rights!"

The other two muttered their agreement.

McCord pointed at the banners.

"I'm not interested in your demonstrations," he said, "as long as you don't block the ring road during the rush hour. If you're daft enough to do that, your main worry won't be our guys but the commuters. Judging by our road rage statistics, many are only one traffic jam away from committing murder."

Judging by their guilty looks, that was exactly what they had had in mind.

"We're homicide detectives," McCord said, finally getting to the point of their visit. "Mrs Keira Lambie was found dead this evening by her husband, and she…"

There was an uproar of voices.

"What?" the woman with the blue hair gasped. "Keira is dead?"

"What happened?" the goatee demanded to know.

The old lady was crying now. "Dear God, sweet little Keira!?"

The shock expressed by the group members seemed genuine, so McCord turned to Boyd.

"Where were you this evening between, let's say, eight thirty and nine thirty?"

Boyd bristled. "What do you mean, where was I? I was here, with my friends, preparing for tomorrow's… event. They can all confirm that."

The group members nodded vigorously.

"Pamela was here, all the time," the old lady said. "I can swear to that on the Holy Bible."

"You still haven't told us what happened to Keira," Boyd said. "How did she die?"

"We can't say at this stage," McCord said.

"But you're asking me for an alibi! What makes you think I had anything to do with it?" Boyd asked. "This is absurd!"

"Not quite," McCord said. "Her last word, as far as we can make out, was your name. And she mentioned about something being proven. Do you have any idea what that was?"

"I haven't a clue," Boyd said, frowning. "Although," she added, "Keira's husband was involved in a dodgy land deal, perhaps that's what she meant."

"Don't you think it's unlikely that this would have been her dying words?" McCord said. "You'd think it would be something more… significant. Like the name of her killer."

"Maybe she was calling for me to help her," Boyd said. "I'm… I was her best friend. I've always looked out for her."

The other group members nodded.

"She did," the old lady piped up.

"Do you have any idea who might have wanted to harm Keira?" McCord asked.

Boyd snorted. "You of all people should know. Look her up in your files! You spend your time persecuting citizens who are trying to save the planet instead of arresting real criminals! I'd like you to leave now; you can see that we're busy."

She pointed to the door.

"Just for the record," McCord said, "we're not persecuting anybody. We are investigating serious crimes, and we are going to leave when I see fit, which is once DS Calderwood has taken all your names and contact details."

"Police state, bloody neo-fascist…" muttered the goatee until McCord's stare shut him up.

"We'll need to get individual statements from you at a later date, but if you can think of anything that might help us find who did this to your friend, then let me know."

McCord put his card on the sideboard, but as he had expected, nobody made a move to pick it up. While Calderwood was noting down the details of the people present, McCord went back into the kitchen. At the door that led out into the garden stood some wellies, walking boots and sturdy shoes, all clean and dry.

Boyd had followed him. "I didn't kill Keira," she said. "You'd better look at the men in her life. Whatever happened, they are to blame."

"You mean the husband as well?" McCord asked.

"If it wasn't the ex, it was the husband," Boyd said. "You're wasting your time here."

McCord was loath to admit it, but he agreed with her.

"Do you know the name of the ex-boyfriend?" McCord asked. "I'm on your side here, remember. I want to catch whoever did this to your friend and see them punished."

"You should have a huge file on him, but knowing you lot, you never made an effort to bring him to justice. He only abused, stalked and raped a woman, of course, and women are not important, are they? You always—"

"His name?" McCord asked, cutting short her tirade.

"Upshaw," Boyd said. "Find Anthony Upshaw."

Chapter 5

A whoop from Calderwood gave McCord's tired brain a much-needed jolt. After they had left the crime scene in the capable hands of the SOCOs and driven back to St Leonard's, his DS had stayed on as well to get the investigation under way immediately.

"I've found this Upshaw," Calderwood said. "About a year ago, Keira Lambie, then Keira McInver, was living in Glasgow. She made a formal complaint there against an Anthony Upshaw, claiming that she left him after a controlling and abusive relationship; after that, he had stalked her. A few months later, when she still refused to return to him, he forced his way into her flat and raped her. There's a statement from Keira's flatmate who found her in great distress when she got home from her shift."

"That must be the guy Boyd talked about," McCord said, sitting up. "What else does it say in the file?"

"The DS dealing with the complaint interviewed Upshaw, who strenuously denied the accusations." He paused. "Oh, but that's weird."

"What is?" McCord asked.

"Upshaw's mother turned up as well and acted as his lawyer. Anyway," Calderwood continued, scrolling down the file, "Upshaw claimed that Keira was lying. He said that he had broken up with her, and because she was angry and upset, she had invited him to her flat and then lied about the stalking and the rape to get back at him. Upshaw made a good impression on the DS, while Keira already had a rap sheet of minor drugs offences. She had no evidence to back up her accusations and no witnesses either." He scrolled quickly down to the bottom of the file. "Case closed."

"Do we have a current address for this Upshaw?"

Calderwood typed a few words. "He is on the electoral register. It's an address in Uddingston; the same one he gave during the police interview. It's about twenty minutes from Glasgow city centre."

McCord jumped up. "Right, let's go then."

"What? Now? To Uddingston?" Calderwood asked, incredulous. "It's past midnight!"

"So? A young woman is dead after somebody broke into her home, and we have the name of somebody whom she accused of stalking, trespassing and violent behaviour!"

"We've got little else, though," Calderwood said. "We can't arrest somebody based on a past complaint that went nowhere and a recent bit of gossip. We have no indication that it was him the neighbours saw hanging around. I think we should get some more background information before we barge in. Also," he continued, seeing McCord putting on his jacket, "an early morning raid on a member of the public without form won't go down well with Superintendent Gilchrist."

"To hell with Gilchrist," McCord said. "I'm going to talk to this Upshaw."

Calderwood made another attempt to reason with his boss.

"Why don't I call this Upshaw first? He might not even be at home."

McCord fumbled in his pockets for the car key. "And warn him that we're onto him? Give him even more time to cover his tracks or disappear altogether? I'm disappointed in you, Calderwood. Where is your hunting instinct? But fine, you go to bed and get your beauty sleep. I'm off to Uddingston, with or without you."

Calderwood sighed and heaved himself out of his chair. "Okay, I am coming. But we must stop to get a double espresso on the way."

McCord smiled. "Deal."

* * *

The roads were quiet, and it took them less than an hour to get to Uddingston. The drizzle, which had stopped before they left Edinburgh, was reasserting itself here.

"I couldn't live in the west," McCord said. "I don't think it ever stops raining here."

Both men squinted up at the modern, well-maintained block of flats on Morag Riva Court. There were still lights on, but the windows on the third floor were dark. McCord pressed long and hard on the button next to the name 'Upshaw'. Both men waited, neither of them speaking. After a couple of minutes, McCord pressed the button again.

"He must be out," Calderwood said, breaking the ensuing silence. "Or he's sleeping the sleep of the righteous."

By now, doubt had crept into McCord's mind, but the thought of a wasted journey irritated him no end. This time, he leaned on the button for several seconds.

"Just making sure," he said, without looking at Calderwood.

There was no reaction, and they had turned to leave, when the intercom crackled into life.

"What?" an angry voice asked.

McCord wheeled round.

"Mr Upshaw, it's the police here. Detective Inspector McCord and Detective Sergeant Calderwood from Edinburgh CID. Sorry to trouble you at this hour, but we urgently need to speak to you."

There was a silence at the other end.

"What about?" the voice asked, all aggression gone.

"Your ex-girlfriend, Keira McInver as she was then. It might be better to discuss this upstairs," McCord said.

The buzzer went, and with a triumphant glance in Calderwood's direction, McCord pushed open the heavy door and hurried up the stairs. In the stale air, there was a smell of cumin and cardamon that reminded McCord of the cherished curry-and-chess nights with his dad. They had done this every Friday for as long as McCord could remember, but recently the sacred event had been hijacked by wedding talk, and his dad was even worse than Clare. Ridiculous!

By the time they had reached the third floor, McCord's mind was back on the case. With a bit of luck, they would arrest the killer now and go to bed.

After their IDs had been examined carefully through the chained door, they were admitted into the flat.

Anthony Upshaw had thrown a bathrobe over his pyjamas and made an attempt to smooth down his unruly curls. He was wide awake now, and his eyes darted from one detective to the other trying to read their faces.

McCord said nothing while he was scanning the shoes in the hallway for traces of mud. There was a pair of white trainers that had grass on them.

"What's going on?" Upshaw asked, showing them into the kitchen and switching on the kettle. "Is Keira alright?"

"Not really," McCord said. "Mrs Keira Lambie was found dead earlier this evening after somebody broke into her home."

Upshaw dropped the mug he was holding onto the kitchen worktop; the handle broke off and slid into the empty sink.

"Keira is dead?"

He slumped onto a chair.

"Yes," McCord said, his tone matter of fact. "Can you tell us anything about that, Mr Upshaw?"

"No," he said, too quickly. "Why?"

"Because Mrs Lambie made an allegation of stalking, breaking and entering and rape against you—"

"That was ages ago, and it was a lie!" Upshaw shouted.

"She also told friends of hers that you had found out that she had moved to Edinburgh," McCord continued, unmoved. "You were following her around again, weren't you? Neighbours of the Lambies saw a man hanging around the house, and we wondered if they might recognise you if we show them a picture."

Upshaw lifted his hands in a defensive gesture.

"I didn't break into her house, and I didn't kill her! You've got this all wrong!"

"That is possible," McCord said, without conviction. "Where were you this evening around eight thirty, nine o'clock?"

"I was here," Upshaw said, "watching telly. And before you ask, I was alone."

"What programme?" Calderwood asked quickly.

Upshaw hesitated.

"Eh, Netflix. The *Game of Thrones* box set."

"Can you show us?" McCord asked, not because he believed this was a credible alibi but because he wanted to see more of the flat.

"It doesn't prove anything, does it?" Upshaw said, stubbornly remaining in his seat.

"Do you mind if we have a wee look round?" Calderwood asked.

"Yes, I do, actually." Upshaw shot up and moved into the hall, blocking the way further into the flat. "Unless you have a warrant."

"We can easily get one," McCord said, "but we would then assume that you have something to hide."

"Well, you'd assume wrong." Upshaw's tone had become aggressive. "I've been falsely accused before, and now it's happening again. You turn up here in the middle of the night interrogating me about a murder I have nothing to do with. I'm sure this is classed as harassment."

Calderwood held up his hand in appeasement. "Mr Upshaw, there is no need to–"

"We didn't say anything about a murder," McCord said with narrowed eyes. "What makes you think that it was?"

"Just… just the way you said it," Upshaw stammered.

McCord made a show of thinking about this explanation.

"Nah," he said after a while. "Mr Anthony Upshaw, I'm arresting you on suspicion of stalking, breaking and entering, and for the murder of Mrs Keira Lambie. DS Calderwood, please read Mr Upshaw his rights and get forensics in here. I want all his clothes and shoes bagged so that we can show them to the witnesses."

"You can't do that!" Upshaw shouted.

He pulled out his phone and pressed a speed dial button. After a few rings, the answering machine kicked in.

"Mum?" he whined, sounding like a child. "The police have arrested me and are taking me to–" he looked at Calderwood, who told him, "–St Leonard's police station in Edinburgh. They think I killed Keira!" He started to sob and ended the call.

Calderwood spoke soothingly to him and made the reading of his rights sound reassuring rather than threatening.

McCord watched his partner trying to calm down Upshaw. Only now did it dawn on him how massive the fallout from this could become. While Upshaw was gathering a few things together for a night in the cells, the men looked at each other. There were no words needed. Calderwood hoped as fervently as he did that they hadn't made a monumental mistake.

Chapter 6

"You did what?" Superintendent Arthur Gilchrist spluttered when McCord briefed him about his night-time escapade the following morning.

"I arrested Anthony Upshaw on suspicion of stalking, breaking and entering, and murder," McCord repeated loudly and slowly as if his boss was deaf or even less intelligent than he judged him to be. "I suppose, I could have made it manslaughter," he added by way of a concession.

"Why was I not consulted? There are proper procedures to be followed!"

Gilchrist was beginning to hyperventilate and took very slow and deliberate breaths.

"Are you alright, sir?" McCord inquired solicitously.

After a few seconds, Gilchrist had regained control over himself.

"I can't believe you did this without my authorisation. Where did this arrest happen?"

"In Uddingston, sir. That's where Anthony Upshaw lives."

Gilchrist closed his eyes. "Uddingston? Good Lord! Please tell me you informed our colleagues in Lanarkshire before barging into their patch in the middle of the night?"

"Time was of the essence, sir," McCord replied. "I believed the suspect to be a potential flight risk."

"Believed? Potential?" Gilchrist was shouting now. "I'll have Archie Crawford, the chief superintendent at Hamilton, on the phone if, no, *when* it comes out what you've done!" He clutched his stomach and screwed up his face in pain.

McCord couldn't care less about the chief superintendent at Hamilton, but he didn't want Gilchrist to end up in hospital, and to be landed with a replacement again who turned out to be worse than Gilchrist himself, although, at this point in time, this seemed hard to imagine.

"You do realise, don't you, that you need reasonable grounds for an arrest, Detective Inspector McCord?" Gilchrist asked hoarsely.

In anticipation of the inevitable confrontation with his superior, McCord had, before the meeting, read up on the definition of the term 'reasonable grounds for arrest'.

"Of course I do, sir. It means that the suspicion must be based on facts, information and/or intelligence, so that a reasonable person would be entitled to reach the same conclusion based on the same facts and information."

Gilchrist's face turned purple. "Are you suggesting that I am unreasonable because I find it disturbing that there's a complete lack of evidence in this case?"

"Forensics are working on that," McCord said, wisely avoiding the question. "Keira Lambie had accused Upshaw of stalking and raping her before, and he had no alibi for last night. I couldn't risk him getting rid of evidence or disappearing."

"Hasn't it occurred to you that he could have already done that on the way back from the crime scene if indeed he was ever there at all? I'll probably have Upshaw's lawyer in here later this morning, making a formal complaint of harassment against us!"

McCord cleared his throat. "Ah, yes, sir, I forgot to mention that Upshaw's mother acted as his lawyer during the previous interview."

"Just when I thought it couldn't get any worse!"

Gilchrist was pacing the floor like a restless tiger in its cage. "Unless forensics have found anything in the flat, you'd better be ready to grovel and pray that this doesn't end in a disciplinary for you. Dismissed!"

McCord made a hasty retreat to his office where Calderwood and PC Surina Dharwan were waiting for him. Calderwood and Dharwan had recently become engaged but refrained from any outward demonstrations of affection; a fact that McCord appreciated. As always, Dharwan was a picture of serenity, while Calderwood asked nervously how the meeting had gone.

McCord waved away the question. "The usual. Anything new?"

"Yes, sir," Dharwan said. "Mr Lambie phoned Wester Hailes police station last night. His wife had told him that she was being stalked. The officer on duty asked if she was in any danger, but Mr Lambie said, no, he was with her, and they would come into the station today to make a formal statement."

"And less than a couple of hours later, she was dead," McCord said. "Why didn't Easton mention that at the crime scene?"

"He's based at Oxgangs," Calderwood said, "so he wouldn't have known about it. He was out on patrol when

Lambie's 999 call came in, so he and his partner were first on the scene."

"What about forensics on Upshaw's clothes and shoes?" McCord asked.

"So far nothing that would make the procurator fiscal happy," Calderwood said. "No weapons, no bloodstained clothes, no muddy trainers."

"Upshaw might not have got blood on him if he chased or pushed her," McCord said, "and he could have cleaned his shoes before we got to him, but there must have been *some*thing in his flat!"

Calderwood flicked through the report.

"One of the SOCOs noted that Upshaw's bedroom was plastered with photographs of Keira Lambie."

"So, he *was* stalking her," McCord said. "That's at least something."

"It's not illegal to display photographs of your former partner," Calderwood pointed out, "but the techies are going to check the dates. Some look as if they were taken on the sly."

"How long had Keira Lambie been married?" McCord asked.

"About six months," Dharwan said. "But she moved in with Lambie in October last year, a couple of months after she moved to Edinburgh. If it was Upshaw who was stalking Keira here, after all this time and despite the distance and her being married, he must have been obsessed with her."

"I suspect he'll deny everything," McCord said, "unless we can at least place him in the vicinity. Any progress with that?"

Calderwood shook his head. "Not yet, but Turner is checking the CCTV in the neighbourhood."

"Good," McCord said. If Upshaw had been in the area at the time of Keira Lambie's death, PC Mike Turner would find out.

McCord's phone rang.

"It's Amy," he told Calderwood and Dharwan as he pressed the green icon and put her on loudspeaker.

"Amy, good morning! Where are you? I would have expected you to be at the station by now, pumping us for inside information!"

Amy, however, was not in the mood for banter.

"I was up until half two this morning looking for this ex-boyfriend, but no luck. Keira deleted all her social media accounts if she ever had any. But that in itself indicates that she was being stalked, doesn't it?"

"Amy–"

"So," Amy went on, ignoring the interruption, "I phoned Donald Murray first thing this morning. Keira never spoke to him about her past, apart from the day when her ex left a card and flowers for her, and she realised he was back. She had a complete meltdown, apparently, and she mentioned his first name: Anthony. Murray doesn't know the surname, but he gave me the contact details of the young guy who always picked her up. He's called Aiden Springfield. He might know more, but he's not answering my calls. I'll get to him today, though."

"Don't bother," McCord said quickly. "The ex-boyfriend's name is Anthony Upshaw. We've already got him in custody."

There was a pause, heavy with disappointment. When Amy finally spoke, there was more than a little anger in her voice. "And it didn't occur to you to tell me."

Calderwood's and Dharwan's disapproval was palpable, and McCord wished he had left the loudspeaker off.

"How was I supposed to know you'd stay up half the night to look for the guy?" he demanded.

"Typical," Amy grumbled, and McCord feared she would hang up on him. He should have known better. Amy's curiosity was always greater even than her irritation with him. "What do you have on him?"

"Keira Lambie accused him of stalking, breaking and entering, and rape in Glasgow last year," McCord said. "But don't get excited; the case was dropped."

Amy gasped. "I hope you've charged him with something?"

"Not a shred of evidence, unfortunately," McCord said. "His mother, who also happens to act as his lawyer, is coming in this morning. Unless he breaks down and confesses, which I very much doubt, we'll have to release him."

McCord heard Amy thumping her desk in fury. "But you can't let him get away with that, surely!"

"We're doing everything we can," he said, angry now himself. "When you've found any proof that he stalked, raped and killed her, do let me know!"

The connection was cut.

McCord stared at his phone, both bewildered and exasperated as he usually was after a phone conversation with Amy.

"That went well," Calderwood said, shaking his head. "Remember she's supposed to be your plus-one. It might be wise not to antagonize her too much before the wedding."

McCord turned to Dharwan for moral support.

"Amy is upset," she said mildly. "She knew the victim; that always makes it harder. It becomes personal. Knowing Amy, she'll go off investigating Upshaw herself now, and I don't think that's a good idea. The best we can do is to focus on solving the case, and quickly."

"You're absolutely right, as always," McCord said. "Calderwood, I have no idea how you managed to hoodwink this extraordinary woman into an engagement. Is Jordan Lambie fit to be interviewed yet?"

"I phoned him this morning," Calderwood said, wisely ignoring the jibe. "He sounded very sleepy. He told me that he has a heart condition and that he is still in shock.

He wondered if we'd mind going to see him. He doesn't feel up to driving."

McCord pulled a face.

"And you, being such a nice guy, agreed, so we have to traipse out to Currie again?"

Calderwood nodded apologetically. "He's staying at the Riccarton Inn while the house is still cordoned off by forensics."

"Why isn't he staying with relatives or friends?" McCord asked.

Calderwood shrugged. "Not sure."

"Poor sod," McCord said. "Not our problem, though. We need to get ready for Upshaw and his maternal lawyer."

Dharwan quietly placed the files she had compiled on the Upshaws on McCord's desk. "Good luck, sir."

* * *

Amy was fuming. If McCord had kept her in the loop, she could have spent the night either in bed or, even better, investigating Upshaw straightaway.

Martin, alarmed by the discord between Amy and McCord he had witnessed, fluttered off to prepare a double espresso and hunt for biscuits.

"These late nights are a killer, my darling," he said, returning with a dainty cup and a plate of milk chocolate hobnobs. "And not just for our complexion; when we're sleep-deprived, we get upset about nothing."

"It's not nothing," Amy said, although the caffeine hit had already lifted her mood. "He should have called."

"He thought you were tucked up in bed while he was out hunting the killer. And he's got him in custody already? What a man!"

"Okay, he's been on the ball with Upshaw so far," Amy admitted grudgingly, "but now he's sitting in his office, twiddling his thumbs until forensics find something. What use was it arresting Upshaw, only to release him again without charge?"

"McCord is doing all he can," Martin said. "His hands are tied. There are regulations—"

"And where are the regulations that protect women like Keira?" Amy asked heatedly. "What is it with McCord, and the police in general, that they can't get a grip on crimes committed against women? Of course, they need evidence, but in order to find it, one has to understand the perpetrator and his motivations."

"I'm sure, they're looking into that," Martin said. "You must leave it to them—"

"The police have let Keira down before. I'm not sitting around waiting for them to get lucky this time."

"Don't go after Upshaw yourself," Martin implored her. "You know what happened before when you followed a man around…"

"Nothing happened," Amy said, although she knew that was not true. "And anyway, I'm only getting background on Upshaw; I'm not challenging him to a duel!"

Martin retreated to his desk with a sigh.

"Fine. Do what you have to do!"

Amy turned to her computer but, feeling his watchful eye on her, looked up and stuck out her tongue at him. He shook his head in mock disapproval.

She lifted her cup.

"Thanks for the coffee, by the way."

* * *

The first thing Amy always did when she was interested in somebody was to trawl through their social media accounts. People's posts, and the photos they were tagged in, often created a picture of their lives.

Going back to the previous year, Amy found hardly any pictures of Anthony Upshaw and Keira together. She wondered why. Happy couples tended to be keen to share their bliss with the wider world. Had Keira's relationship with Upshaw ever been happy? Or had he tried from the very beginning to keep her hidden – an unnoticed, helpless victim? Perhaps Keira, battered and bruised, had been unwilling to be in the public eye herself?

To Amy's surprise, since the spring, Upshaw had been in a new relationship. The woman in question, Louise Braithwaite, lived in an upmarket area of Lanark with her parents and an Old English Sheepdog called Dudley.

Instead of documenting her latest purchase or evening out, many of Louise's posts invited donations for the various charities she supported. In most of the pictures, she was outside and wore casual clothes and wellies.

Clearly, beauty and glamour were not something she possessed, but she had a much more precious quality – an infectious smile that made her instantly likeable. She was often in the company of friends and animals who equally seemed to dote on her.

Upshaw had documented their lives meticulously, with frequent posts of meals and outings together. Amy noticed that in his posts, it was always the two of them, nobody else. The photos had a staged quality about them, as if Upshaw was trying to show off his girlfriend to the outside world.

Something struck Amy as odd about the more recent posts. As she was going through them, she thought for a moment that the screen had jumped back because the pictures were somehow familiar. Then it hit her. Upshaw had slightly altered previous pictures and re-posted them with comments suggesting they had been taken later.

Puzzled, Amy went back into Louise Braithwaite's feed. From June onwards, there were no more pictures of her and Upshaw, and she had changed her status to single again, while Upshaw's still stated that he was 'in a relationship'.

Amy felt her nose twitch. Had she just discovered another of Upshaw's stalking victims? Did Louise

Braithwaite realise the danger she was in? She needed to speak to her. Amy reread Louise's most recent post that had today's date on it.

Louise Braithwaite was due to help at a 'Brew and Blether' session for the elderly and lonely in a church in Glasgow's east end at midday. Amy checked the time on her phone. If the traffic wasn't too bad, she could make it.

She looked across to Martin, who seemed engrossed in one of his articles, and quietly made her way to the door when he called her name. "Where are you going?" he asked suspiciously.

Amy whirled round.

"I'm having lunch with a girl. At a church. Nothing to worry about. See you later!"

Martin leant back in his chair with a frown. "A girl? At a church?"

But he got no further explanation – Amy was already halfway down the stairs.

Chapter 7

The lunchtime traffic had been worse than Amy had expected, and by the time she rushed towards the entrance of St Andrew's East Parish Church, sweating in the unseasonably warm September sun, the last parishioners were tottering out of the door of the community hall.

"You're too late," a stooped old man said to Amy, waving his walking stick disapprovingly. "Louise could have done with some help earlier. We had to wait for ages to be served. The biccies are all gone, but there were no nice ones anyway. And each week the tea gets weaker."

"You can always make your own," Amy retorted, swallowing the 'ungrateful git' that was on the tip of her tongue, and to the sound of indignant huffing followed by a rant about the disrespectful youth of today, she entered the hall.

The inside felt cool and dark after the bright sunshine outside. Louise Braithwaite and the minister were clearing away cups and plates. From their slightly bedraggled looks, Amy suspected they were ready for something stronger than a cuppa.

"So sorry, but the session is finished," the minister said. He was concentrating on lifting a heavy tray without the stacked cups toppling over.

Then he looked up and took in Amy's appearance.

"Oh. I take it you're not here for the Brew and Blether," he said. "What can I do for you?"

"A wee blether with Louise, actually. If you don't mind," she said, turning to the young woman.

Intrigued, Louise Braithwaite eyed up Amy, and it was obvious that she had no clue what this might be about. The minister moved gingerly towards a door at the back, his arm muscles straining. "I'll just finish up in the kitchen, Louise, and then I'll be in the office if you need me."

The women sat down at one of the long tables.

"I must apologise for waylaying you like this," Amy began. "I'm Amy Thornton, and I work with *Forth Write* magazine. You might have heard about us?"

Braithwaite's eyes brightened. "I knew I had seen you somewhere before. You are the journalist who solves crimes with that detective inspector, Mc-something…"

"McCord," Amy said. "That's right. Police resources are always stretched, so I'm helping him to investigate this case as well. You'll have heard about what happened in Currie last night?"

Braithwaite shook her head. "I don't even know where that is."

"On the outskirts of Edinburgh," Amy said.

"There hasn't been a murder, has there?" she asked, genuinely shocked. "I'm sorry, but I have no idea how I can help you with this."

"A woman called Keira Lambie was killed," Amy said. "Does the name ring a bell?"

Braithwaite frowned. "No, should it?"

"The police have Anthony Upshaw in custody," Amy said. "I'm sure you remember him."

"Anthony? Under suspicion of murder? No!"

She had raised her voice, and before she had finished, the minister stuck his head through the door.

"Everything alright, Louise, love?" he asked.

Amy was sure that he had been eavesdropping and gave him an indignant look. She wanted Braithwaite to speak freely, and in her experience, the presence of a man of the cloth was not always helpful.

"Thanks, I'm fine, Matthew," Braithwaite told the minister. "I was just surprised."

She turned back to Amy, and the minister reluctantly withdrew.

"Matthew is a darling," Louise Braithwaite said in a whisper, "but he does like to know what's going on. Now, what is this about Anthony being a murder suspect?"

"Keira Lambie, the victim, made a complaint against Anthony more than a year ago… for stalking her after she left the abusive relationship, and raping her."

Louise Braithwaite clapped her hands over her mouth. "Oh, my God. I had no idea. Are you sure?"

"Did he never mention a previous girlfriend?" Amy asked.

Braithwaite shook her head. "He never wanted to talk about past relationships. I asked him once, but he said, 'it doesn't matter what was in the past; I don't need to know what you have been up to either.'"

"I bet he wasn't keen to give you chapter and verse of what he had done," Amy said drily. "But I had hoped you might be able to help me… and the police."

Perhaps it was the mention of the police that jogged Braithwaite's memory and overcame her reluctance to speak ill of her former boyfriend.

"I'm not sure if this has anything to do with this, but once I found a box of pictures of a girl, and asked him who she was, but he only said it was a crush he had had long ago. I assumed it was when he was at school because she looked so young. Do you think that was her, this Keira?"

Amy nodded. "Probably. I don't have a picture of her to show you, unfortunately. About a year ago she moved to Edinburgh to get away from Anthony."

Braithwaite sat down, raking through her memories as if she didn't trust them anymore.

"If all this is true, why was he not prosecuted?" she asked.

"The original case was dropped," Amy said. "Lack of evidence. But Keira told friends in Edinburgh that her ex – we assume that was Anthony – had tracked her down and was stalking her again. Last night, somebody broke into her home and killed her."

"How awful," Braithwaite said, genuinely appalled. "And the police really think it was Anthony? I find that very hard to believe."

Amy tried to hide her disappointment. "You and he were an item for a few months. Was he ever violent towards you?"

Braithwaite's answer came without hesitation. "No, never. And he hasn't been stalking me either since we broke up."

"So, if you don't mind me asking, why did you break up?"

Braithwaite stroked the torn paper of the tablecloth. "I was the one who ended it. I didn't feel loved," she said.

"He made a great fuss of me at the beginning – took me out a lot, introduced me to his mother and so on – but then he started working longer hours at the factory because they were short-staffed."

Amy was quite moved by Braithwaite's innocence. She would have bet a month's salary that Upshaw's 'overtime' consisted of travelling to Edinburgh to follow Keira Lambie around.

"It wasn't the only reason, though," Braithwaite went on. "I felt that he wasn't really interested in me at all. Which is quite understandable," she added with a modest shrug. "I'm not a very exciting person. But still, I felt I deserved better."

Amy waited until Braithwaite's clear blue eyes met hers.

"Of course you do, Louise," she said firmly. "How did Anthony take the break-up?"

"Not very well," Braithwaite said. "He pleaded with me, begged me to reconsider, cried even, but… I don't know how to explain it… it was as if it wasn't the loss of *me* that upset him, but the loss per se. I'm sorry if that doesn't make any sense."

"It does," Amy said, "if he was always obsessed with Keira, and only used you as a replacement."

Braithwaite gave a bitter laugh. "Not very flattering, is it? But now that you mention it, his mother was all over me. She was so keen for us to get engaged. I thought it was quite sweet at first, but now I wonder…"

"…if she just wanted her son settled with a suitable girl to keep him out of trouble," Amy said, finishing the sentence for her.

"It's possible," Braithwaite said, "but it's only guesswork, isn't it? Who knows what goes on in somebody else's mind? If he really did all those things, I had no idea he was capable of that." She shuddered. "I hope it's not true, I really do."

Matthew, the minister, appeared in the doorway. "I feel so bad," he said. "I haven't even offered you a refreshment.

Not very Christian, is it. The biscuits are all gone, I'm afraid, but there's some nice lemonade in the fridge."

"That's very kind of you, Reverend, but I must be going," Amy said. "Thank you, Louise, for talking to me."

"I'm sorry I couldn't be of more help," Braithwaite said.

"You're going to have a drink, though, Louise?" the minister asked. "I feel we deserve it."

Amy deduced from Braithwaite's knowing smile that the pastor would soon be grilling his lamb.

The sky had clouded over when Amy stepped out into the yard, and despite it being no more than eighteen degrees, it was clammy, and the MG was hot and stuffy inside. She started the engine, opened all the windows and drove off towards the M8, thinking over what Louise Braithwaite had told her.

She had hoped to establish a pattern of behaviour with a credible witness, but no such luck. On the plus side, it had confirmed, at least in her mind, that Upshaw had been obsessed with Keira Lambie for years. And she guessed that this obsession would not have stopped with Keira's death. If she judged him correctly, he would return to the scene of the crime as soon as he was released, and she would be waiting for him.

Chapter 8

Dharwan's file on the Upshaws had made interesting reading. Early on in her career, Mrs Patricia Upshaw had acquired a reputation as a ball-breaking prosecutor, but after the premature demise of her wealthy husband she had taken early retirement. Perhaps his absence had removed the need she felt to persecute others.

Anthony, their only child, had enjoyed an expensive but undistinguished education at the High School of Glasgow and scraped through a Business Diploma course from City of Glasgow College. Straight afterwards, he had begun working at the Tunnock's factory in Uddingston where he dealt with the shipping of their famous teacakes and caramel wafers.

Now, with Anthony in trouble and her reputation again under threat, Patricia Upshaw had morphed into a formidable defence lawyer. Her son being in a prison cell was not a situation she was prepared to tolerate, and she made this very clear from the outset. Superintendent Gilchrist had invited her into his office before Anthony Upshaw's interview, hoping to avert the danger of a formal complaint against his department by wearing his uniform and an obsequious smile.

Patricia Upshaw, however, declined the offer of a seat and remained standing. Everything about her appearance whispered wealth and unassailable good taste. Lest Gilchrist forgot she was a woman with clout as well as style, she placed her expensive leather briefcase on his shiny, uncluttered mahogany desk with a thud that made him wince.

"I do understand that your people are *trying* to do their job," she said to Gilchrist, completely ignoring McCord, "but as a lawyer, I can tell you that my son's arrest is a textbook example of how *not* to run an investigation, and I demand that you release him immediately. I can tell you categorically that you are wasting your time and resources investigating him."

Gilchrist was about to reply when McCord butted in.

"There were reasonable grounds for arrest," he insisted. "The victim had made serious accusations against Mr Upshaw before, and up to the day of her death, she expressed a fear of him to her husband and several colleagues.”

Patricia Upshaw peered at McCord over her Ray Ban glasses with the expression of a teacher about to reprimand a pupil for speaking out of turn.

“Irrelevant on both counts. The historic case against my son, to which you are referring, was dropped, and, thankfully, an individual’s feeling does not yet determine another person’s guilt.”

“Some cases are dropped because there isn’t enough evidence, not because the allegations are false,” McCord said, ignoring Gilchrist glowering at him.

“There was no evidence for the simple reason that Anthony hadn’t done anything,” Patricia Upshaw said sharply. “And that’s why the girl withdrew the accusation.”

The surprise on McCord’s face was not missed by Patricia Upshaw.

“You didn’t know she had done that?” She tutted. “In future, you need to do your homework, Inspector. But,” she continued with a condescending smile, “I don’t blame your colleagues or anybody else who fell for her lies. She was a great little actress, and I suppose children with such a difficult start in life learn how to manipulate people. It’s a defence mechanism, according to an article in the *Journal of Applied Psychology*, which I read at the time.”

Gilchrist nodded sagely as if every day he pondered the behavioural complexities of disturbed young people.

Patricia Upshaw looked at McCord, expecting him to acknowledge her superior knowledge in this matter, which he didn’t. With an air of resignation, she continued.

“That girl latched on to poor Anthony, who was far too naïve to see what was going on even though he was quite a bit older than her. She was destitute when they met; just out of care, hardly any qualifications, no prospects, and Anthony had a nice flat and a decent income. My son saw himself as her knight in shining armour, I suppose.”

"So, why didn't they live happily ever after, then?" McCord interrupted her.

Patricia Upshaw was not thrown off course so easily.

"Eventually, Anthony saw through her and ended the relationship," she said. "But she couldn't accept losing her golden goose, and out of revenge, made up all sorts of allegations against Anthony. If he was guilty of anything, it was being too kind and too much in love."

Gilchrist's warning glance prevented another vocal outburst from McCord whose flared nostrils spoke volumes.

"As far as you know, Mrs Upshaw, when was the last time your son saw Keira Lambie or was anywhere near her?" Gilchrist asked gently, as if inquiring after a parent's health.

"In August last year," Patricia Upshaw said without hesitation, "when that ghastly business was finally settled. You can ask him."

"We will," McCord said, unable to stop himself, "amongst other things."

"Please yourself," she said blithely and then, turning to Gilchrist and picking up her briefcase, "Shall we get this over with?"

Gilchrist opened the door for her and glared at McCord, daring him to upset her any further. As they walked down the stairs towards the interview rooms, Gilchrist commented on the unseasonably warm weather and, having procured an agreeable response from Patricia Upshaw, tilted his head towards McCord. 'That's how it's done', the gesture said. McCord's expression remained impassive until Gilchrist resumed his charm offensive towards Patricia Upshaw, and only then did he roll his eyes.

Calderwood had taken Anthony Upshaw to Interview Room 2 and had set up the recording. As the small party entered, he rose and greeted Patricia Upshaw with his genuine smile, but it bounced off an impenetrable wall.

Patricia Upshaw sat down beside her son on one side of the Formica table. She made a show of opening her briefcase and taking out a notebook. Refusing to be intimidated, McCord and Calderwood took the seats opposite. Gilchrist settled himself on a chair in the corner. Since he was not familiar with all the details of the case, he had, albeit very reluctantly, allowed McCord to conduct the interview.

"Mr Upshaw, when did you last see Mrs Keira Lambie, née McInver?" McCord began.

"I haven't spoken to her since she… we broke up," Upshaw said.

"See?" his mother said. "Exactly as I told you. Can we go now?"

"Not just yet," McCord said. "You didn't answer my question, Mr Upshaw. You might not have spoken to Mrs Lambie, but you certainly saw her and left a message and flowers at the zero-waste shop where she volunteered. We also have witnesses who saw a young man hanging around the street where she lived. That was you, wasn't it?"

Patricia Upshaw glanced at her son in surprise but recovered quickly.

"Definitely not," she said. "Why would he? My son has had a new girlfriend for the past few months."

Upshaw shifted uncomfortably in his seat.

"Name? Address?" McCord asked Upshaw, but his mother butted in again.

"Her name is Louise Braithwaite, a very nice young lady, daughter of a colleague of mine. There's no need whatsoever to involve her in this."

"Actually," Upshaw said, lifting his chin, "Louise and I have split up."

Patricia Upshaw lost her countenance only for a split second. "Never mind. It is immaterial. The important point is that my son had moved on from the relationship with that unfortunate girl. The other question you should be asking," she continued quickly, "is the how. As you well know, my son lives in Glasgow and has a full-time job there, so how could he have been over here in Edinburgh to stalk her? The very idea is absurd."

"Not at all," McCord said. "Mr Upshaw, your flat is only a few minutes' walk from Uddingston railway station. It provides a regular train service to Curriehill. From there, it is only a five-minute walk to Caulderhame Road, where Keira Lambie lived… and died," he added pointedly. "A colleague of mine is reviewing the CCTV as we speak. It'll look much better for you in court if you voluntarily admit to being there before we present you with the evidence."

McCord had barely finished the sentence when Patricia Upshaw cut in. "He'll do no such thing."

"I'll do no such thing," Upshaw echoed, his expression blank.

McCord shrugged. "As you wish. Do you own a car, Mr Upshaw?"

"A VW Golf."

"Registration?"

"SL70 PHZ."

McCord registered the faint smile around the corners of Upshaw's mouth and decided to tell Turner to concentrate on the train connection.

"And how did Mrs Lambie react to the card and flowers you left for her at the zero-waste shop?" he asked Upshaw.

Before her son had a chance to reply, Mrs Upshaw spoke again. "May I point out that even *if* my son was foolish enough to be snared again into a relationship with that girl, and *if* you were to find evidence of that, which I very much doubt, it is not illegal to send somebody a card and flowers."

"It is if it is unwanted, repeated, and causes the recipient fear and alarm," McCord said. "It's called stalking, which is a criminal offence. I thought, as a lawyer, you'd know that."

Gilchrist was out of his chair as if stung by a hornet, but before he could say anything, Mrs Upshaw had also risen, her eyes blazing. "You have failed to present any evidence for your vague suspicions, Inspector, so I am going to take my son home now."

She carefully slid the unused notebook back into the briefcase and held Gilchrist's gaze until he seemed to shrink inside his uniform. "And if any of those ridiculous accusations end up in the press, I'll hold you personally responsible," she told him.

"There won't be any need for that," Gilchrist hastily replied. "If my officers were a little over-zealous, it was with the best of intentions, I can assure you. Thank you so much for coming in and clearing up a few things for us."

He shook hands with Patricia Upshaw and her son, and ushered them outside.

"Why didn't you tell me that Keira Lambie had dropped her complaint against Upshaw?" McCord snapped at Calderwood when the door had closed. "I came across like a right numpty."

"I'm sorry," Calderwood said, blushing. "I must have missed that. We were in such a hurry to get Upshaw–"

"You mean, *I* was in such a hurry," McCord said. "Never mind. I wonder why Keira Lambie, or McInver as she was then, dropped her complaint. It is possible that she had made it all up and realised she wasn't getting anywhere. But maybe somebody put pressure on her. When did Keira move to Edinburgh?"

"Straight afterwards," Calderwood said. "She registered her new residence three days later as a flat in Edinburgh."

"That tells me she was still frightened of Upshaw – or his mother, which wouldn't surprise me. She spoke about Keira as if she was something the cat had dragged in. And you wouldn't want Mrs Upshaw as your enemy, would you? Gilchrist barely restrained himself from curtsying."

Calderwood laughed. "While you barely restrained yourself from cursing."

"I was a very good boy," McCord said, pulling out a tenner. "Now you be a good boy as well and get us a coffee from across the road, while I'm going to pay our resident genius a visit."

Chapter 9

DC Heather Sutton was not a team player, recoiling from even the most innocuous human contact, and yet, she was Edinburgh CID's most precious asset. Without ever questioning McCord's instructions, she sneaked her way into any suspect's online transactions and brought to light whatever they thought was safely hidden from view.

Both kept this arrangement quiet. Sutton, out of a disinclination to speak to anybody apart from McCord; and McCord, because it would be the end of both of their careers if some of her trawls through the Internet became public knowledge.

Still, even the few instances that the other officers knew about had earned her the nickname 'Heather the Hacker'. She was fiercely loyal to McCord because he allowed her to work the way she preferred; in solitude behind a multi-layered barrier that only McCord breached when the need arose. And today was such a day.

"Sutton, please check Keira Lambie's financial transactions going back to the time she was Keira McInver and living with Anthony Upshaw. See if there is anything unusual. His mother indicated that he was supporting her financially, and I'd like to know if that is true and to what extent."

Sutton merely nodded. Her eyes, hugely enlarged by the thick lenses she was wearing, never left the screen, and she didn't utter a single syllable because there was no need to.

With a quiet 'thank you' that probably went unheard, McCord withdrew and walked over to a bleary-eyed Turner, who was sitting at his desk, staring at CCTV footage.

"Anything useful?" McCord asked.

Turner, glad of a rest, paused the CCTV and patted a pile of printouts. "I found a guy in a hoodie matching the neighbours' description walking past the primary school round the corner at half past six on the day of Lambie's death."

"Good work!" McCord said, picking up the sheets.

"Not good enough," Turner said. "He always kept his head down, and I haven't got a later sighting of him. Lambie wasn't killed until 9pm; that's one and a half hours later."

McCord examined the grainy pictures and swore under his breath. "That could be anybody. Maybe Superintendent Gilchrist's press conference this afternoon will get us some more witnesses."

"Is he going to mention Upshaw?" Turner asked.

"Not a chance," McCord said. "He's afraid Mrs Upshaw is going to sue the pants off us anyway. No, it's going to be a general appeal for information. The official line is that we are looking for a burglar who was hanging around the Lambies' house in the past few weeks. I'm not holding my breath, but you never know. Do we know yet how Upshaw travelled to Currie? By car or by train?"

"I haven't managed to do that yet," Turner said.

"Then take another officer to help you. We need unequivocal proof he was there. If we can at least prove the stalking, we might be able to make a manslaughter charge stick as well."

When Turner had gone off to liaise with a colleague, McCord decided to check on the progress of the door-to-door inquiries among the Lambies' neighbours in Currie.

"Something and nothing," said the PC who had only shortly returned from his second trip to Currie. "I talked to a few people who were out when we first went round the street. Several neighbours saw a man of Upshaw's height and build hanging around there on separate occasions, but none of them could identify Upshaw without a doubt. He always wore a hoodie that covered most of his face, and he made tracks soon as anybody walked towards him."

McCord tried not to let his frustration show.

"Okay, thanks, write it up."

More hopeful, he made his way across to Dharwan. "Any more on Keira Lambie's background?" he asked.

Dharwan called up the file she had compiled on the computer. "Born Keira McInver in 2005 in Glasgow, father unknown. Taken into care at the age of four when the mother died of a drug overdose. Moved in with Anthony Upshaw in 2021. Was working as a barista at Costa in August 2023 when she went to the police about him. As soon as the charges were dropped, she relocated to Edinburgh. Lived in a bedsit for a couple of months, then moved in with Jordan Lambie in October. They married in January this year."

"That was quick," McCord said. "Shotgun wedding?"

Dharwan shook her head. "Her medical records show no record of a pregnancy."

"Anything else?"

"She kept a very low profile in Edinburgh," Dharwan said. "No wonder, if she was hiding from Upshaw."

"I'm going to speak to the members of The Green Fist," McCord said. "We'll start with the ones Amy mentioned and ask them to come in tomorrow. Keira Lambie might have confided in one of them. We also need to find out what the marriage was like. Under normal circumstances, the husband would be our number one suspect, and I haven't ruled him out by any means. Has the phone come back from forensics?"

"Yes, but our colleagues are still working through all the communications. It'll take a while."

"And Jordan Lambie? Anything interesting on him?"

"No previous convictions, not even a parking ticket," Dharwan said, while she clicked on his file. "Born 1998, one sister; MA in Environmental Science; married 2019, divorced 2021."

"That's ridiculous," McCord said. "He was only a kid!"

"He was twenty-three," Dharwan pointed out. "That's only one year younger than I am now, and I'm getting married soon."

McCord was mortified. "That's completely different," he blustered. "After all, it's Calderwood you're getting hitched to, and there is no better man far and wide."

Dharwan smiled. "I know."

"Talk of the devil," McCord said as Calderwood through the door and handed him a coffee. "Thanks, I'll have that on the way. It's time to find out what Mr Jordan Lambie has to say for himself."

* * *

The Riccarton Inn in Currie was a whitewashed, two-hundred-year-old hostelry towering over the main road. McCord suspected that the interior designer had been given the impossible brief 'cosy yet contemporary' but had failed to achieve either. Still, the ambience was pleasant, and the mouth-watering smells made McCord regret not coming earlier and taking the opportunity of a nice pub lunch.

Jordan Lambie was waiting for them in the bar area, and once everybody had ordered and paid for their drinks, they sat down in a quiet corner.

Tall and lanky, Lambie reminded McCord of a thin, straggly tree that might snap at any moment. His face was pale with the deep shadows under dull, sunken eyes, and McCord thought that he had seen better-looking corpses.

At the age of twenty-six, Lambie was a widower with two marriages and a divorce under his belt. McCord was mystified by people who found it so easy to commit, but then, here was a prime example of how it could end. A wreck of a man who should have been in his prime.

"I hope you're feeling better?" Calderwood asked solicitously.

Lambie shrugged but did not answer.

McCord's heart sank. The lunchtime traffic all the way through the city centre had been murder, and he had hoped for a slightly more loquacious witness. Or suspect.

Calderwood tried again.

"We're very sorry for your loss."

Lambie nodded but still said nothing.

"Could you please take us through last night's events?" McCord asked, losing patience.

"Every little detail might help us find the person who did this to your wife," Calderwood added. "You phoned the police last night about a stalker. Did you see him then?"

"No, I've never seen him, b-but she t-told me during our d-dinner that Upshaw was b-back." Lambie's face contorted as if he was in physical pain. He took a sip of his Coke. "Sorry, it g-gets w-worse w-with stress."

McCord resigned himself to a long, painful session.

"Take your time, Mr Lambie," Calderwood said gently.

Lambie's facial muscles relaxed a little and his stutter became less pronounced as he went on.

"Thank you. When Keira and I met, she told me that she'd had an ex-boyfriend who abused, stalked and then raped her. The police didn't take her seriously, so she left Glasgow and made a new start in Edinburgh. But she was still scared of him. She had deleted all her social media accounts and told nobody where she was going. She was all alone in the world and had nowhere to stay after she ran out of money and her landlord chucked her out. I said she could stay at my place until she found somewhere she could afford. We fell in love and got married soon after."

"Are you able to tell us about last night?" Calderwood asked.

"Keira and me had been out at The Balerno Inn–"

"Why not here?" McCord interrupted.

"We wanted something a bit special," Lambie said, lowering his voice so that the barman could not overhear, "and when we g-got b-back, I w-went into the study…" Lambie's stutter had returned with a vengeance, and his voice faltered as he began to cry.

"Take your time," Calderwood said again.

Lambie wiped away the tears. "Then I heard her scream and ran into the living room; she was lying on the floor. There was blood everywhere, and she didn't move. The kitchen door was open, so I ran outside but I didn't see anybody. Then I called 999."

"Did your wife say anything?" McCord asked.

Lambie stared at him uncomprehendingly. "She was dead!"

"No, she wasn't," McCord said. "She tried to tell the ambulance driver something, but he couldn't make sense of it."

Lambie shook his head. "I couldn't find a pulse, she was dead!"

"She must have been unconscious from the fall and then regained consciousness while the other driver was dealing with you," Calderwood suggested.

"That bloody useless heart of mine." Lambie closed his eyes. "What did she say? His name? It must have been him!"

"No, she said something about 'proven'," McCord said, watching him closely. "Do you have any idea what she could have meant?"

Lambie shook his head. "No idea, unless…"

"Yes?" McCord leaned forward.

"She could never prove what Upshaw did to her, and that's why all this has happened, isn't it?"

He started to cry again.

Calderwood looked at McCord for approval, and he nodded.

"I think you should rest now, Mr Lambie," Calderwood said. "We might need to speak to you again when you're feeling better. In the meantime, if you can think of anything else, do give us a call."

McCord put his card on the table.

They left the inn and made their way to McCord's Juke that was sitting in the car park and had heated up in the sun.

"He's not exactly a James Bond villain, is he?" Calderwood said.

"No, but there are several things that I don't get," McCord replied. "Why would Keira's last words be about a past allegation? Why not, as Lambie suggested, tell us the name of the person who killed her?"

"Maybe she tried," Calderwood said, "and wanted to tell us that the allegations against Upshaw were true even if they were not proven."

"Then there's something else that's been bugging me. Why would they light a fire on a summer's evening? It was mild, and they're young, not two old pensioners who need an ambient temperature of twenty-eight degrees."

Calderwood shrugged. "Perhaps they put on the fire for… romantic purposes?"

"Romantic…? Ah," McCord said, cottoning on eventually. "And what about her being followed? Did she not notice the stalker until that evening?"

"No, it was before that," Calderwood said. "Amy told us that Keira was afraid of somebody when she was with the group, remember?"

"Why then didn't Keira tell her husband that she was being stalked until that dinner? Would she not have said something as soon as she knew that Upshaw was back?"

"You're right, it is strange she didn't confide in him earlier. Maybe the Lambies had problems in their marriage?"

"Exactly my thoughts," McCord said.

"Even if they had, it doesn't mean that he killed her," Calderwood pointed out.

"No, but since we're in the area anyway, let's have a chat with the staff at The Balerno Inn and see what they made of the Lambies' little tête-à-tête."

Chapter 10

The Balerno Inn was easy to find. Driving slowly along Main Street in the small village west of Currie, McCord immediately spotted the neat lettering on the solid limestone walls. Window boxes bursting with flowers and a carefully maintained front garden told the potential customer that this was a classy place for a meal or an overnight stay.

Inside it was quiet. There were no customers, only a barman wiping the tables and putting the condiment trays away.

McCord made the introductions and asked to speak to whoever was on duty the previous night.

"That would be Jackie," the barman said, pointing to a stout, middle-aged woman who was having a bowl of soup and a sandwich in the corner. "The others are off today I'm afraid."

The woman called Jackie had put down her spoon and was looking at them expectantly.

"We're sorry to disturb your lunch," Calderwood said as they sat down at her table, "but we need to ask you a few questions, Ms…"

"Reeves. But Jackie will do fine."

Two bright eyes examined them with undisguised curiosity, and McCord was hopeful that they had found a witness who was switched on.

"Are the rumours true then?" Reeves asked. "Keira Lambie was killed last night?"

"Did you know her?" Calderwood asked, taking out his notebook.

"I knew of her," Reeves corrected him. "There was a big hoo-ha when people heard about the plans for the solar farm her husband was planning. Some folks who have horses in the fields were upset at the possibility of having to relocate them and the scenery being spoilt, and The Green Fist were up in arms as well, so nobody was happy apart from the people who made a packet by selling their muddy fields to Lambie. But now it's likely to fall through anyway, I hear."

McCord's knee began to bounce up and down. "That's not exactly relevant to why we're here, Ms Reeves. I understand that Jordan and Keira Lambie were having dinner here last night. Did you serve them?"

"Jackie. And yes, I did," Reeves said. "But tell me first what aspect of their dinner would be relevant to your visit, Inspector?"

She looked McCord straight in the eye. A nippy sweetie, McCord thought.

"Did you have the impression that they–" McCord hesitated; he didn't want his question to be too obvious "–got on?"

Reeves grinned. "No need to be coy. You want to know if Jordan Lambie gave the impression that he was about to murder his wife? No, he didn't. In fact, I had the impression that he was trying to make up after a fight."

"Did you hear what the fight was about?"

"I'm not in the habit of listening in on other people's private conversations," Reeves said pointedly. "And I was too busy anyway. But they talked very… intensely for a while. Well, he talked a lot. He seemed to be pleading with her, but she was not convinced."

"And then?" McCord asked.

"Then she started to smile and agreed to something. He was one happy bunny and took a selfie of them. They were holding hands, and he ordered a bottle of sparkly. And not the cheap fizz either. The real McCoy. They talked some more. Then, he shouted 'what?' really loudly – all the other guests stared at him. He pulled out his phone, went out and made a call. I was in here, so I didn't hear what it was about."

"That must have been when he phoned Wester Hailes about the stalker," McCord said to Calderwood, pleased to have found a credible witness at last. "Go on, Ms… eh, Jackie," he corrected himself.

"That's better," Reeves said with a flirtatious smile. "She was suddenly in a hurry to get home; they didn't even order desserts. But if they made up after a fight, I suppose they wanted to be alone." She winked at McCord. "If you get my drift."

McCord didn't react, wondering if he was imagining things or if the woman was actually coming on to him. Usually, females were wary of him; they always fell in love with Calderwood with his ridiculous good looks and manners. He would ask him later.

"Strange, though…" Reeves continued thoughtfully.

"What?" McCord asked, remembering why he was there.

"She looked happy but also… stressed somehow. I'm sorry, I can't explain it any better. It was just a feeling I had. Poor girl. She seemed nice, and so young, too."

McCord rose from his seat. "Thank you. You've been very helpful."

"Anytime, sweetheart," she said, stirring her cooling soup suggestively.

Motioning at Calderwood to follow him, McCord fled.

* * *

When McCord and Calderwood had finally lurched their way back through the afternoon traffic, Dharwan was waiting for them in great anticipation; not so much of the return of her fiancé but of McCord because she was desperate to tell him about Keira Lambie's phone records.

"There were no threatening messages on her phone," Dharwan said, "but for twenty-four hours before the evening of her death, she did not use her phone at all. There were some messages from her colleagues from the café, and quite a few from members of The Green Fist."

"Who from?" McCord asked. "Amy said something about a guy walking her home all the time, Aiden or something."

"Yes, I've found him. He's called Aiden Springfield. He tried to contact her five times the day she was offline."

"Seems a bit extreme for a fellow tree hugger," McCord said. "Maybe they were hugging without trees being involved?"

"There's nothing explicit," Dharwan said. "He only asked her if she was okay. The leader of the group, Pamela Boyd, was also concerned. They usually chatted quite a lot. The last message before Keira went offline was from her, asking if Keira had 'swapped it'. Keira replied, 'I can't'. No idea what that was about."

"And from the husband?"

"Lots of messages in general, asking if she was okay, where she was—"

"Is that not a bit over the top?" McCord asked.

"Lambie knew what a terrible time she'd had," Calderwood said, "and if they had a falling-out, he would want to show her that he cared."

"But there were no messages from him on the day she was offline, so he wasn't worried about her then," Dharwan said.

McCord frowned.

"Odd. Maybe she was at home. Or he knew she didn't have her phone. Nothing there to incriminate the husband, anyway."

"That's good, though, isn't it?" Calderwood asked. "It confirms what we were thinking all along. It was Anthony Upshaw."

"Thinking won't do," McCord said. "We need evidence. Have forensics come up with anything at all?"

"Nothing to tie Upshaw to the actual crime scene," Dharwan said. "And judging by Turner's face, he hasn't had a breakthrough with the CCTV either."

McCord's phone pinged. He looked at the screen and jumped up. "Sutton."

He rushed over to her fortress and weaved his way in.

"Please tell me you've got something," he said before realising this would only confuse her. Why would she have sent a message otherwise?

"I've got something," she said obediently but was clearly annoyed at the meaningless preamble she had to endure. "Keira Lambie paid Anthony Upshaw no rent but spent all her money on food and bills."

"So, he gave her a home but wasn't keeping her like the mother suggested. Not exactly a knight in shining armour, our Anthony. But it doesn't really help us." He tried to suppress his disappointment, but even Sutton had noticed it.

"No. But it was your idea," Sutton said, "not my fault."

"Of course not," McCord hastily agreed. "Thank you."

He turned to go.

"A thousand pounds was paid into Lambie's account just before she moved to Edinburgh."

McCord wheeled round.

"What? Where from?"

"Patricia Upshaw."

"Now, that is very interesting," McCord said. "Very interesting indeed."

Chapter 11

Amy had parked her mother's MG round the corner from Caulderhame Road, allowing her to observe everybody entering and leaving the cul-de-sac, which had never experienced such footfall. Most of Currie's population, it seemed, and some from further afield, had come to pay their respects or simply gawp at the scene of Keira Lambie's tragic demise, quite possibly to contemplate their own comparatively good fortune in the face of catastrophic events in the lives of others.

Amy herself was not immune to such feelings, but today her presence had a nobler purpose: to observe the man who was to blame for a young woman's misery and death, and who, in all likelihood, would evade punishment unless she intervened.

She had phoned Calderwood for an update on Upshaw's interview before setting off, in case McCord had managed to keep him under lock and key, but as she had suspected, the mills of justice were grinding so slowly they could be seen as being at a standstill.

From Calderwood's account of the mother, Amy concluded that Patricia Upshaw would not allow her son to go anywhere near the crime scene, but Amy was convinced that he would find a way to come back to the place where Keira had died.

Her phone lay in her lap, ready to be picked up should she need to take a furtive picture or pretend that an urgent message had made her stop. Keeping her eye on the road, where the stream of ghouls was thinning, she mindlessly chewed the cheese and tomato sandwich she had bought from the Co-op in the retail park and took a big swig of water. She had let the windows down, but the air outside was heavy with impending rain. Desperate for a coffee, she had to make do with a bar of dark chocolate because she didn't want to risk missing Upshaw. Her back began to ache from the long wait, and she felt the beginning of cramp in her right leg.

There were hardly any people on the pavement now, and doubts began to creep into Amy's mind. Had she been wrong about Upshaw's need to come back to the scene of his crime? Or was he just more careful than she had given him credit for? Then a terrible thought occurred to her. What if the cul-de-sac had a footpath at the other end that might have allowed Upshaw to sneak in and out unseen by her? With a very unladylike curse, she swung open the car door and slid out of the low-lying chassis. A satisfying stretch loosened up her spine, and the tingling in her leg subsided. She locked the MG and walked purposefully across the road. That way, she would look like all the other nosey parkers rather than somebody on a stake-out.

To her great relief, the other end of Caulderhame Road was blocked all the way by a high fence, so she turned back and stopped outside the Lambies' front garden, which was cordoned off with blue-and-white crime scene tape. People had left bunches of carnations and freesias still in their cellophane wraps, some of them with notes covered in cling film to protect them against the unpredictable weather.

> *The Sugar Bun will never be the same without you. RIP.*

There were several signatures and kisses. Colleagues from the café where Keira had worked, Amy guessed.

She was struck by a collection of beautiful golden, purple and white chrysanthemums; stapled to the broad, black ribbon around their stems was a card. She bent down to read Donald Murray's effusive and emotional message; white was a symbol for Keira's innocence, gold for her preciousness, and purple for the fight for women's rights. Amy was gratified that he hadn't deemed the black ribbon worthy of an explanation as well. Dwarfed by Murray's contribution was Pamela Boyd's bunch of garden herbs. Tied with raffia ribbon, their intoxicating fragrance suffused the humid air. Her much shorter farewell was written on a biodegradable card with embedded wildflower seeds.

Humbling all the other tributes, however, was a huge bouquet of blood-red roses, displaying their glory unfettered by any packaging or ties. Amy lifted each carefully to avoid being stung by the thick, sharp thorns, but there was no message. She wondered who it was from. Keira's husband? Aiden Springfield? Perhaps even twisted Anthony Upshaw, which would mean that she had indeed missed him and was wasting her time waiting for him. She pulled herself upright, now uncertain how long she should hold out.

The sultry afternoon had given way to a clammy evening with puce clouds piling up in a quickly darkening sky. Sudden gusts of wind lifted the first dry, brown leaves off the ground, swirling them around in the light of the streetlamps as if trying to bring them back to life.

A middle-aged woman emerged from two houses down the road. Amy gave her a sympathetic smile, poised to start a conversation about the Lambies, but the woman regarded her with an expression of faint disgust, probably suspecting Amy of being brought here by the lurid sensationalism of the quickly spreading social media posts. The woman added her modest bunch of flowers to the others and, with a bowed head, mumbled a prayer. After an almost inaudible 'amen', she dabbed her eyes and returned home.

Amy was surreptitiously taking a couple of photos of the tributes when the pool of light she was standing in flickered and then extinguished. Suddenly, she stood in semi-darkness. Uneasy, Amy realised the cul-de-sac was now deserted, and the blocked exit, at first so welcome, now felt like a trap. She made for the safety of the car when she saw a hunched, hooded figure coming towards her. Amy froze, blood thundering in her ears, but the man walked straight past her, seemingly oblivious to her presence. Being much shorter than him, she caught a glimpse of his face. Fleshy lips and a weak chin – it was Anthony Upshaw, his features distorted in pain. Clasping the car keys in her pocket, she forced herself not to run. Back at the MG, it took her trembling fingers a couple of seconds to insert the key. She yanked the door open, slipped into the driver's seat and pushed down the small side lever on the passenger door to lock herself inside. Relieved, she slumped back into the cool leather. Breathing slowly in and out to calm her thumping heart, she waited for Upshaw to re-emerge.

Not for the first time, she cursed the fact that she drove a car that made heads turn wherever she went. It also didn't help that she was parked right under a streetlamp which was working. Typical. What should she do next? The safest bet would be to disappear before he could link the car to her. But then she would miss him on the way out, and she wanted a picture of his car as proof that it really was him. Hoping he would be just as oblivious to his surroundings as before, she reversed the car a few metres into a darker spot under a sizeable beech tree.

After what seemed an age, Upshaw reappeared. Amy dived into the passenger seat, hoping he hadn't noticed her, and pretended to look for something on the floor. When she slowly lifted her head to peek out of the window, he was running along the road towards the northern edge of the village. Had he seen her? Had he guessed what she was doing here? No matter. She started the engine and slowly followed Upshaw down the hill.

There were no cars parked here, and the houses had given way to trees on either side of the road. Where was he going? Then it dawned on her. The railway station! She had seen a sign on the main street but not understood its significance. She took a note of the time: half past eight. She drove up to the platform as far she could. There were only two tracks, and before she had decided whether to get out of the car or not, the four carriages of an electric train appeared from the east and screeched to a halt. Less than a minute later, it left for Glasgow.

Deciding it was reasonably safe now, Amy abandoned the car where she had stopped, jumped out and ran towards the platform. It was empty, and Upshaw was nowhere to be seen. Exhaling loudly, Amy stood for a moment, relishing the release from the tension she had been feeling for hours. A rumbling of thunder on the distant horizon made her turn back to the car. Hopefully, she would make it home before the storm broke.

As she set off, she weighed up the success or failure of her mission. She had no irrefutable evidence that it was Upshaw who had returned to the scene of the crime, but she had seen him with her own eyes. She had found out how he got to Currie, which would make it much easier for McCord's team to find evidence that he had been in the area at the time of Keira Lambie's death.

Passing the turn-off into Caulderhame Road, Amy had a sudden feeling that she should see if Upshaw had left a message, even if it seemed unlikely. She stopped abruptly, got out of the car and rushed across to the Lambies' garden. Lying in a pool of darkness underneath the extinguished streetlamp, the place seemed even creepier than before. Amy pressed the torch icon on her phone and scanned the tributes along the fence. She could see nothing that had been added, but she couldn't shake off the feeling that something was missing. As the beam travelled again from left to right, she realised what it was. The glorious bouquet of roses had gone. Amy was sure that Upshaw hadn't been carrying anything when he left. So where were they? Slowly, she moved the torch, scanning the surrounding area. There! She let the light linger on the same spot. Her mind racing, she took a couple of photos and pressed McCord's number on speed dial.

"Amy?"

She registered with some satisfaction that McCord always answered in a flash when she called him. "I'm in Currie," she told him, "and–"

"What are you doing there? I've told you–"

"I'm doing what your guys should be doing," Amy said irritably. "Upshaw came back to the crime scene tonight. He was wearing a hoodie, but I recognised him anyway. He took the half past eight train back to Glasgow, so get Turner to check the CCTV at the station for the evening of the murder."

"Thanks, I'd never have thought of that," McCord said, and as always, his sarcasm exasperated her. But he didn't give her a chance to vent her anger, being furious himself. "What were you thinking following a potential stalker, rapist and murderer around on your own in the dark? He could have attacked you!"

"At least I got some results," Amy shot back.

"What results?" McCord had raised his voice now. "Upshaw is, sadly, a free man, and him visiting the place where his former girlfriend died is proof of absolutely nothing."

Tears pooled in Amy's eyes. "Stop patronising me! I'm trying to protect people who are in real danger!" she shouted.

There was a moment's silence on the other end. "Who is in danger?" McCord asked.

"Jordan Lambie, Aiden Springfield or whoever left these!"

She killed the call, opened a message to McCord and attached the picture of the roses flung violently over the neighbour's hedge, the delicate petals scattered on the immaculate lawn.

Chapter 12

As soon as he got out of bed the following morning, McCord knew it was going to be a quagmire of a day that would stretch into the distance without any hope of a breakthrough. The Lambie case was going nowhere fast, as was his best man's speech, which was weighing him down like a ten-ton boulder round his neck.

"I think marriage as an institution should be abolished," he said in reply to Calderwood's cheery 'good morning' when he entered the office. "What's the bloody point?"

Calderwood smiled. "Still working on your speech, then?"

"There is nothing to work on!" McCord complained. "My dad loves Clare, and she loves him. I love my dad, so I'm happy for them. End of story. What is there to speechify about?"

"It's an important day when two people commit to each other," Calderwood said. "It's a celebration of a love that hopefully lasts for the rest of their lives."

"I get the distinct feeling it's shortening mine," McCord said. "Between the prospect of this wedding and

Gilchrist first thing this morning lecturing me again on proper police procedures, I'm losing the will to live."

Gilchrist had not been happy about the complete lack of progress in the case, not helped by the final forensics report that contained nothing whatsoever that would allow McCord to arrest anybody. To top it all, Amy was in a huff with him for pointing out the bleeding obvious, and if she decided she was not coming to the wedding with him, he might as well find a plot to bury himself in.

"Aiden Springfield is waiting downstairs," Calderwood said, dragging McCord away from the morass of his self-pity. "Shall I send him up?"

McCord sighed. "I suppose you'd better. Maybe he knows something we've missed."

Calderwood grinned. "It says on his Instagram bio that he's a poet. Maybe he can give you some inspiration for your speech?"

"Ach, shut up, Calderwood, and get him in here."

* * *

Aiden Springfield reminded McCord of a bunny rabbit he had once been given to hold at Gorgie Farm when he was a wee boy. Their primary teacher had decided to introduce the feral children of Niddrie's mean streets to the wonders of nature, and sure enough, the newborn lambs on their wobbly feet and the massive, pink sow with black spots that was impassively suckling her frantic litter had made the children exclaim in delight.

What had fascinated McCord the most, though, was a little rabbit whose dark brown fur was almost black and the softest thing he had ever touched. The helpless creature seemed perfectly content to lie in his lap and be gently stroked by his index finger. McCord still remembered the acute sense of loss when the keeper took the rabbit off him and put it back into the pen.

McCord glanced at Springfield, who, in his judgement, was congenitally incapable of hurting anybody, and suddenly the thought of Upshaw destroying the roses worried McCord even more.

Springfield had the cautious movements and intense gaze of an introvert. His black T-shirt and batik trousers looked as if they had been randomly retrieved from the bottom of the wardrobe, and there was an aura of sadness about him, which was probably part of his nature but exacerbated by the loss of Keira Lambie.

"You loved her, didn't you?" McCord asked without any preamble.

If Springfield was surprised at this unconventional method of questioning, he did not show it.

"Yes," he said simply.

"Was it you who left a large bunch of red roses at the Lambies' fence?" McCord asked.

Springfield nodded. He didn't ask how this was relevant, and McCord found himself disarmed by this lack of defensiveness.

"Was it common knowledge that you were in love with Mrs Lambie?" McCord asked.

Springfield lifted his shoulders in an almost imperceptible movement. "I suppose people guessed. I never said anything to anybody."

"Not even to Mrs Lambie?"

"I told her, of course," Springfield said.

There was no 'of course' about it as far as McCord was concerned, and he found himself envying this man who was so sure of himself and his feelings.

"And did she return your affections?" McCord asked.

"No," he said. "If she had, she would still be alive."

"What makes you say that?"

Springfield fixed his large, doe-like eyes on McCord.

"I would have taken her away somewhere, anywhere, to keep her safe from that animal Upshaw, but she was loyal to her husband even though he was not much better than him."

McCord sat up. "What do you mean?"

"He didn't really love her; he tried to own her. To control her." Springfield looked at McCord for confirmation that he understood how terrible that must have been for the woman he loved. "He kept her like a bird in a gilded cage."

"Was he ever violent towards her?" McCord asked.

"Not in a physical sense. Keira said that Jordan had saved her when she came to Edinburgh, given her a home, a safe haven, a new start. They loved each other and he was wonderful, she said, and she owed him everything. I told her that love doesn't keep a tally; love only wants the happiness of the other person, nothing else."

"So, lately, she was not happy in her marriage?" McCord asked.

"Her husband tried to restrict her movements, keep her at home. He even tried to forbid her to attend meetings of the group!" Springfield said, stretching out his arms.

McCord suspected this was the closest to outrage that Springfield ever came. Yet, he could well imagine that Jordan Lambie was not keen on a group whose leader was a vocal opponent of his business plans and also contained a dreamy poet serenading his pretty wife.

"Did Mrs Lambie ever tell you that she was afraid of her husband?" McCord asked.

"No, but I knew. He was beginning to show the same traits as her ex-boyfriend. She feared that the man who used to protect her was turning into a control freak, and it would start all over again. When I walked her home, she always asked me to leave her at the corner so that her husband wouldn't see me. I asked her why he didn't pick her up, and she said she hadn't told him about her ex stalking her."

"But why wouldn't she tell him that?" McCord asked. "If he was so protective of her, surely he would have done something about Upshaw?"

"She said he would just try to keep her at home all the time. In his opinion, home was the only safe place for her, and they had everything because they had each other. He was suffocating her. That is also a form of violence. But she told me not to worry; she would not allow him to harm her. The problem was that he was doing that already."

"Why didn't anybody in the group encourage her to go to the police when she told you all that she was being stalked again?" McCord asked disapprovingly. "We might have been able to gather some evidence and put Upshaw or whoever it was away before it came to this tragedy."

"We all did, especially Pamela, but even she could not persuade her. Keira didn't have any faith in the police," Springfield said with mild reproach. "She said she had tried in the past but for somebody like her, there was no justice."

"So, you believed her story that she was stalked by Upshaw and that he forced his way into her flat and raped her before she left Glasgow? Maybe you are unaware that she later withdrew her accusation?"

Springfield's eyes widened in horror. "Upshaw raped her? She never told me that."

His voice had become a whisper, and McCord wondered what hurt Springfield more: the knowledge of what Keira had suffered or that she had not confided in him. Springfield closed his eyes as if trying to communicate with her beyond the chasm that separated them. Suppressing his natural impatience, McCord waited until Springfield had processed this new information.

It took a while, but then Springfield nodded. "She knew how worried I was about her already and didn't want to burden me further. Keira was the kindest person I've ever met."

Springfield's eyes filled with tears, and McCord swiftly moved on.

"Were you not concerned when Mrs Lambie was offline for more than a day?"

"I was," Springfield said. "I sent her several messages."

"We know that," McCord said. "But, given the circumstances, would you not have tried harder to make sure she was alright?"

A single tear ran down Springfield's cheek, unchecked.

"I had told her I loved her the day before and suggested we run away together, but she said no – she valued me as a friend, and all the other things people say in those situations to soften the blow."

Springfield's breaths became shallow, and McCord feared the poet was about to cry in earnest, so he swiftly wrapped this up.

"Thank you, Mr Springfield," he said. "Before you go, I wanted to make you aware that Upshaw turned up at the Lambies' house yesterday and destroyed the flowers you had left."

Springfield did not seem surprised.

"Men like him destroy everything that is beautiful," he said. "They can't help it."

"When were you there?" McCord asked.

"Yesterday morning around eleven."

"Good," McCord said, relieved. "At that time, Upshaw was here being interviewed, so he doesn't know for sure that the roses were from you. But he might have observed you and Keira together before and concluded that you were lovers."

"Being jealous would fit with his possessive nature," Springfield said. "I'm sure he is incapable of understanding true love."

"We don't know exactly what motivated him to destroy the roses," McCord said, "but he was obviously very angry. So, until we have enough evidence to arrest him or know more, please be on your guard."

He handed Springfield a photo of Upshaw they had taken from his Instagram account.

"That's him."

Springfield glanced at the smiling face and recoiled.

"Here's my card," McCord said. "If anything, and I mean *anything*, happens in connection with Upshaw, even if you just see him from a distance, I need to know about it. Day or night. Note down the place and the time; if you can, take a picture."

Springfield dropped the photo on the desk but kept the card, twisting it nervously in his long, delicate fingers. "I so wish Keira had come away with me," he said quietly.

So do I, McCord thought.

He accompanied Springfield out of the building and watched him walk towards the bus stop. The air was crisp after the thunderstorm the previous night, and fluffy white clouds danced across an azure sky. He was desperate to escape for an hour or two to Musselburgh Lagoons, but there was no time for that, and the migrant birds from the Arctic hadn't returned yet anyway. As soon as this case and the wedding were over, he promised himself, he'd go there.

* * *

Back in his office, he had barely sat down when his phone buzzed.

It was his dad.

The little angel on his right shoulder wrung his hands. His father had never called him at work before; it had to be something serious. But the little devil on his left whispered with a malicious grin, 'Perhaps the wedding has been cancelled?'

McCord tapped the green icon.

"Everything okay, Dad?" he asked breezily.

"Never better," Keith McCord said. "Sorry to bother you when you're on duty but I just had to tell you that we picked up the rings today. From Clare's shop, of course, so we got them at price. Good going, eh?" He chuckled.

"Cheapskate," McCord said, smiling at his father's boyish enthusiasm.

"Clare is so excited about the wedding, and if I'm honest, me too. How's the speech coming along, Russell?"

McCord's smile faded.

"Fine, eh, Dad, sorry, but I must get back to work. Killer to catch."

"Of course, son, mustn't keep you. Only wanted to put your mind at rest about the rings. You can pick them up any time; just give us a buzz."

"Will do, thanks, Dad."

He hung up and went across to Mike Turner's desk.

"Are we any closer to placing Upshaw at Keira Lambie's house the evening she was killed?" McCord asked him.

"I've been through all the CCTV from the station," Turner said. "He arrived with the 3.50 train from Glasgow."

"Is it definitely him?"

"Yes, he must have been hot in his sweatshirt; he pushed the hood down and wiped his forehead. See?"

Turner showed him a still. Curly hair, fleshy lips and weak chin –there was no doubt it was Upshaw.

"Good. That confirms the neighbours' accounts. But what we need is evidence of him leaving after Keira Lambie died."

"No joy there, I'm afraid," Turner said. "Couldn't make a positive ID at any time. There was a rugby match on at Malleny Park between the Currie Chieftains and Glasgow Hawks – around 2,000 at the match – and for the 18.14 back to Glasgow, the platform was jampacked full of people, most of them young men in hoodies. It was raining by that time. It's quite possible that he was amongst them but…"

The young constable hung his head, but the expected outburst of frustration from his boss did not materialise.

"It's just one of those days," McCord said, exhaling in resignation. "At least, Upshaw can't claim that he was in

Currie for the rugby match; he arrived far too late. So, he is still in the frame."

"There are no other cameras between the Lambies' house and the station," Turner said, "but I could widen the search. He might've got himself some food if he was hanging around for hours."

"Good thinking," McCord said. "Try the retail park first – I saw a few fast-food joints there – and then the café further along the main road."

Turner sighed.

"I know it's boring," McCord said, "but we need to nail this guy." If only to stop Amy from doing something stupid, he finished the sentence silently.

Returning to his office, he found Calderwood bravely battling with a teetering pile of paperwork.

"Calderwood, see if you can get this Pamela Boyd to come over and talk to us again."

"Will do," Calderwood said. "Any particular reason?"

"It seems that she and Keira Lambie were quite close. Boyd seems to blame men for every evil in the world, but perhaps she has a slightly less romantic view of our victim than Springfield."

"But do you really think that Keira Lambie had something dodgy going on in her life? Everybody says she was a lovely person."

"She might well have been, but I'm not sure that she was the saint that Springfield makes her out to be. At the very least, she was lying to her husband about going to the group, and she didn't mention to him that Upshaw was after her either until that last dinner. Springfield makes Jordan Lambie sound like a monster, but then again, he would, seeing that he was head over heels in love with his wife."

"Talking of relationship issues," Calderwood said with a cautious glance at his boss, "why don't you phone Amy and let her know that you acted on her information and warned Springfield about Upshaw?"

"Don't be ridiculous, Calderwood," McCord said. "The last thing she needs is encouragement, or she'll be off dating this Upshaw next. One of these days, she'll get hurt with her crazy schemes, and I couldn't live…"

He broke off.

"She might be more inclined to listen to you if she feels that her efforts are appreciated," Calderwood said. "I don't think she understands how you feel about her."

"I don't think she wants to understand," McCord said. "It's pretty obvious, isn't it? You've always known, even before I did myself."

Calderwood shook his head. "She needs to hear it from you."

"And what if all she wants to do is to play detective?" McCord asked. "Do you seriously think she would be interested in me if I wasn't a DI?"

Calderwood shrugged. "You'd have to ask her. But you *are* a detective, aren't you? Body and soul. And not many women would understand that. Amy does. In her own way, she is just as crazy as you are. You are a perfect match, can't you see?"

McCord stared at his partner.

"Are you kidding me? Amy and I a perfect match? The woman drives me insane! All we ever do is fight! By all accounts, the Lambies were a happy couple once – now one of them is dead. I shudder to think what a bad match is like! Marriage is a minefield!"

"And what about your dad and Clare?" Calderwood asked. "Maybe you shouldn't be their best man if you feel like that about the wedding."

"That's completely different," McCord said. "They *are* a perfect match. They fit together like two pieces of a jigsaw. And you and Dharwan might make it as well if you're lucky."

Calderwood gave an ironic bow.

"Thanks for the vote of confidence."

Chapter 13

When Calderwood had phoned Pamela Boyd, she had readily agreed to come to St Leonard's but made it clear from the start that she was only cooperating to get justice for her dear friend Keira who had been a victim of the patriarchal and misogynistic attitudes that pervaded society as a whole, and the police force in particular.

Watching her stride along the corridor towards him, McCord knew that here was another woman who was not easily cowed, but who, unlike Mrs Upshaw with her defensive hostility, thoroughly enjoyed a good fight. Conversations broke off and heads turned as she left the duty sergeant in her wake, approached McCord and stretched out a firm hand to shake.

"I hope you have made some progress in the case, DI McCord," she said by way of a greeting, and he caught himself wishing he had better progress to report.

McCord was not surprised that Pamela Boyd had emerged as the leader of the environmental group and had changed it from The Green Fingers to The Green Fist. Today, away from her covert, nocturnal activities, she wore flowing, wide-legged linen trousers and an ethnic cotton smock, proving that elegance could be ecologically and morally sound.

"Thank you for coming in, Ms Boyd," he said. "I'm glad I don't have to visit you in a cell to conduct this interview."

Boyd smiled. "Your colleagues were surprisingly sensible this time."

He made an inviting gesture towards his office where Dharwan was waiting for them. Facing a lifelong feminist and eco-warrior, McCord had deemed it safer to have a female ally present.

"Pamela, please," Boyd said, shaking Dharwan's hand as well, no doubt appraising her rank and level of oppression. "I take it you have not arrested and charged anybody yet in connection with Keira's death?"

"We are still gathering evidence," McCord said, "and we were wondering if you could shed some light on Mrs Lambie's relationship with her ex-boyfriend and her husband."

"There was no 'relationship' with Anthony Upshaw," she said sharply. "Soon after they got together, he started to beat her; when she finally found the courage to leave him, he stalked her, broke into her home and raped her. She went to the police, but the system let her down, just as it has thousands of other women."

Boyd stopped, clearly expecting a comment from McCord.

"My understanding is that there was no evidence at the time," he said, "and that Keira withdrew her statement a few days later."

"Because she knew that the odds were stacked against her. Keira was too vulnerable to fight."

"Do you know what happened after she left Glasgow?" McCord asked.

"She came to Edinburgh to escape from Upshaw, but, unfortunately, he tracked her down, and the stalking began again."

"Did you witness any of it yourself?" McCord asked.

"It started with an anonymous card and flowers that were left at the shop one night. It seemed harmless enough, but Keira immediately knew they were from him, and she was terrified. She broke down and later told me all about her ordeal."

"Did you not encourage her to go to the police?"

"Believe it or not, I did, despite my own very negative experiences with your colleagues."

Dharwan had briefed him about Boyd's record of public disobedience, and McCord was not about to apologise on behalf of the force.

"I take it that Keira refused."

"Of course she did," Boyd spat. "She had already been let down once. She felt there was no point going through the added humiliation of being disbelieved all over again."

"The case was only closed after Keira withdrew her allegations," McCord said. "Did she tell you that she received a thousand pounds from the Upshaws before she moved?"

"She did," Boyd said. "But the money was from Upshaw's mother, not him. She tried to get Keira out of the way, so that her son could get away with his crimes. Did you know she is a lawyer? That woman should be prosecuted herself."

"Perhaps she didn't believe Keira and simply did what any mother would do to protect her son?" Dharwan suggested.

"She enabled his crimes," Boyd said, her cheeks colouring with fury. "And he probably killed Keira. Happy now?"

"You say 'probably'," McCord said to deflect Boyd's wrath away from Dharwan although his colleague seemed unflustered by the sudden attack. "Do you have doubts about Upshaw's guilt?"

"Well, he is not the only man who made Keira's life a misery, is he? Keira certainly picked them."

"You mean her husband? We were told that they had a happy marriage," McCord said.

Boyd snorted. "I'm sure *he* was happy – playing the great protector but, in fact, controlling her. Did you know that Keira didn't tell him about Upshaw being back?"

"Yes," McCord said. "Do you know why?"

"Because she was afraid that he would use it as an excuse to imprison her completely at home, that's why. He tried to stop her from attending meetings of our group, even from working. Sometimes it feels like we're back in the nineteenth century. Thankfully, with my support, Keira stood her ground and told him she would keep working at the café. But she didn't dare tell him that she was still meeting us. She needed a friend to make her see what kind of man she had married, but for some unfathomable reason, she remained loyal to him. He did not deserve it. He did not deserve *her*."

"Maybe she saw a different side to him," McCord said. "They were seen in The Balerno Inn drinking champagne, having a good chat, taking a happy selfie and then rushing home together. To the waiting staff there, she didn't give the impression at all that she hated him."

Boyd looked confused. "They had champagne? And took a selfie?"

McCord nodded.

"But you have your own reasons for disliking Jordan Lambie, haven't you?" he asked. "You campaigned against his plans for the solar farm. Explain that to me. I thought that the Greens supported renewable energy projects."

"We are not the Greens," Boyd said contemptuously. "Like everybody else, they have fallen into the trap of believing that replacing one kind of destructive technology with another is going to stop climate change. It won't. Some of them in that party even work with the government and have bowed to the pressure of the conglomerates who profit from the destruction of our planet."

She held McCord's gaze, challenging him to contradict her, but he had no intention of doing so.

"You must be delighted, then, that Lambie's project has been abandoned while he is being investigated for not following the correct legal procedures," he said.

"Not following the correct legal procedures?" she mimicked him derisively. "That bastard was about to ruin our countryside with panels filled with heavy metals and poisonous chemicals. The carbon footprint of solar panels is horrendous. Most of them are produced in China by slave labour, while polluting the rivers there. And that's supposed to be progress? Men like Lambie leave a trail of destruction wherever they go. I'm sure he'll wriggle out of it in the end. His kind always does."

McCord felt a headache coming on. Somehow, they had veered off the topic of Keira Lambie and ended up in Boyd's world of eco-warfare. "Was Keira not conflicted then, with her husband building solar panels and you, her friend, campaigning against it?"

"Keira meant well and did an awful lot for the local community: bird boxes, litter picking, rewilding and so on. She, like some others in the group, had not quite grasped the urgent necessity of direct action, but she would have got there in the end."

"One last thing," McCord said. "Keira went offline for the whole day before her death. Do you know why?"

Boyd shook her head. "I was worried. I thought she might be unwell with the bug that is going round, but I never imagined anything like this would happen. If I'd known…"

"Her last message to you was that she couldn't swap something. What was that about?" McCord asked.

Boyd didn't hesitate a second. "Oh, that. I'd asked her to switch some files into a different format, but she didn't manage to do it. Sad to think that the last contact I had from her was about something so trivial, isn't it? Well, I do hope you do better than your colleagues and put both Upshaw and Lambie behind bars. For a very long time."

McCord rose. "We'll do our best. Thank you for coming in" – he couldn't bring himself to use her first name – "Ms Boyd."

* * *

"Do you know how many women are being stalked in Scotland?" Amy asked Martin fiercely, as if it was his fault. "Listen to this: 'According to the Scottish Crime and Justice Survey from 2019, over a quarter of women aged sixteen to twenty-four reported experiencing at least one form of stalking and harassment.' A quarter! And over 50% of the cases that come to court are linked to domestic abuse. I don't even want to think about what happened later during the various lockdowns."

"I know, but I hope you will also mention in your article that men are also victims. Not as often as women, but still…" Martin said.

"True," Amy admitted, "but the real worry is how many stalkers are getting away with it. You should read the transcripts of the interviews I've done with those poor women. They're living a nightmare, and they all feel completely powerless. Many of them have even contemplated suicide. God, sometimes I hate men, and I hate the police!"

"Now, now," Martin said, twittering in alarm. "Do remember that most men are decent people and that fine detectives, like DI McCord, do their level best to protect women from abuse and violence."

"Perhaps," Amy conceded grudgingly, "but it's still not good enough. The case we're working on at the moment is a perfect example of how women are failed by the system. This Anthony Upshaw needs to be taken out of circulation, along with his mother." She raised her voice in frustration. "Can you believe she is covering up for him?"

"He is her son," Martin said and got up to make her a calming cinnamon latte. "I wish I hadn't suggested writing this article. It's putting you in a very negative frame of mind, and you simply must stop blaming poor DI McCord for the failings of lesser men. Why don't you research something more uplifting, for example" – he pretended to rack his brain for ideas – "yes, that's it, the best wedding venues in Scotland!"

"My research is not a form of personal therapy," Amy said irritably. "I'm a serious journalist, and what I think of McCord is neither here nor there."

"Oh, but it is," Martin said. "In a couple of weeks, you'll be attending his father's wedding together."

"What has that got to do with anything?" Amy demanded.

"We know since our first perusal of Jane Austen's divine *Pride and Prejudice* that such events bring lovers together," Martin said. "When I think about it, the title is quite an accurate reflection on you both."

Amy snorted. "No, it most certainly is not. Although, now that you mention it, I wouldn't say no to a date with Colin Firth in his wet shirt." Seeing Martin's dreamy expression, she burst out laughing. "And neither would you."

Chapter 14

Donald Murray was all jovial charm as he joined McCord for a chat in the office. He even attempted to flirt with Dharwan, who had brought him upstairs, but he was met with a wall of professional courtesy. Undaunted, he shook McCord's hand cordially.

"Thanks for coming in, Mr Murray. Please have a seat."

"Donnie, please," he said with a winning smile. "Delighted to be of assistance."

McCord always ignored witnesses' suggestions of over-familiarity, and he made no exception in this case. He was sure that Murray was trying to endear himself to anybody who might be useful to him now that he was facing an investigation into his involvement with illegal practices. He wouldn't be flavour of the month with the locals either for surreptitiously selling his land to Jordan Lambie.

"We're trying to find out more about Keira Lambie and her claim that she was stalked by Anthony Upshaw," McCord began.

"It wasn't a claim, it was the truth," Murray said emphatically. "Poor Keira was terrified of him."

"Do you have any evidence of him stalking her?" McCord asked. "Pictures? Handwritten notes? Anything?"

"Unfortunately not," he said. "If he had left anything, I would have given it to the police, but he was too cunning. He only left an anonymous card and flowers when he first turned up in Currie. Keira binned them straightaway, and as far as I know, he didn't send anything else, but Keira told us that he followed her around."

"Did she actually see him? Did he ever approach her?"

"She didn't give him the chance. Keira only went out to go to the café where she worked and to come to us. Whenever he could, Aiden made sure he was there to go with her. Aiden Springfield, that is, one of our members."

"I know, we've already spoken to him."

If Murray was miffed that he was deemed less important to the police than Springfield, he did not show it.

"Was there anything going on between the two of them?" McCord asked.

Murray shook his head.

"I doubt that very much. Aiden would have liked that, but Keira was quite immune to other men's advances."

McCord deduced from Murray's expression that his own had been firmly rebutted, too.

McCord eyed the would-be Casanova with mild distaste. "You had some… business dealings with Jordan Lambie. Did he ever talk about his wife or his marriage?"

"No, Jordan never talked to me about his private life. We only met a couple of times and exchanged a few emails about the land sale. Which I assumed to be perfectly within the rules, by the way," he added earnestly. "I had no idea what Jordan had done, and I desperately needed the money for my daughter–"

"I'm not interested in planning permission issues," McCord interrupted him. "All I want to know is if the Lambies had a happy marriage or not."

"Our Great Leader didn't think so," Murray said with some venom. "She was always on to Keira about freeing herself from her oppressive husband. A bit rich coming from her; she never got anybody to marry *her*."

"I take it you are referring to Pamela Boyd?"

"Of course. I think she was simply jealous of Keira."

"Jealous?" McCord asked, surprised. "Why?"

"Because Keira was becoming very popular with the members of the group. Not all of us agree with the hard line Pamela has taken, and Keira was kind, a good listener, great with IT, and a real fighter when it came to the crunch."

McCord frowned. "I had the impression that she was quite a timid, vulnerable person."

"Being scared of a man who stalks you doesn't mean you're timid; it means you're smart. No, Keira was quite determined never to be abused again by anybody."

Since Murray hadn't mentioned the rape, McCord assumed that he didn't know about it. It was understandable that Keira confided in Boyd, rather than her would-be lovers. "So, you don't think Keira was afraid of her husband?"

Murray shrugged. "Keira told me once that he didn't want her to come to the group, which I understand, what with Pamela agitating against his development plans. Keira didn't want a fight, so she asked us not to say anything should he phone, and she always made sure to get home before him."

"That sounds as if he put her under a lot of pressure," McCord said.

"Silly of the guy," Murray said, shaking his head. "Despite her lack of education, Keira was a bright young woman. She couldn't stay at home all day; she needed company and something worthwhile to do. Perhaps he was simply worried about her health and wanted her to take it easy. When she first came, Pamela had a rant about the villains in the pharmaceutical companies, and Keira mentioned that she was taking supplements because they were trying for a baby."

"From what you're saying, it doesn't sound to me as if they were about to split up," McCord said. "And we have other witnesses who say that they seemed close on the evening she died. Well, thank you, Mr Murray. If you can think of anything else that might help us, please get in touch."

* * *

After Murray had left, a despondent McCord told Calderwood about the conflicting and unhelpful statements of Green Fist members.

"It is interesting that Murray's story differs from Boyd's and Springfield's," Calderwood said. "I wonder if he has something to hide beyond the land sale."

"You mean, perhaps he didn't take 'no' for an answer when Keira rejected him?" McCord asked.

"I'm not sure. Surely, Keira would have told Pamela if he had molested her, and she would have done something about it."

McCord nodded with a grin. "Definitely."

"I've been thinking about what Amy said right at the beginning," Calderwood said, "so I got in touch with Upshaw's line manager at Tunnock's biscuit factory and cross-referenced his work times with sightings of the hooded man in the Lambies' area."

"Good idea," McCord said. "And?"

"Upshaw wasn't at work during those times, but that doesn't prove that he was the hooded man."

"What about the photos of Keira that were found in his flat?" McCord asked.

"The techies have confirmed that they all date from the time she was still in Glasgow, so they can only be connected to the previous accusation of stalking, and that was withdrawn by Keira herself."

"Damn," McCord said.

"I've also been to the café where Keira Lambie worked," Calderwood continued. "Everybody there seemed shocked and distraught at the news. Keira was very popular with her customers and colleagues, and the only complaint her boss had was that she didn't work full-time for him."

"Did Kiera not mention anything about Upshaw to them? Or the husband for that matter?" McCord asked.

"She mentioned to them that she was being harassed by an ex-boyfriend and asked them not to give out any information about her whereabouts to anybody, but she had never spoken to them about problems in her marriage."

McCord banged the desk.

"We're not getting anywhere. Upshaw looks to be our man, but how did he manage to break into a house, cause a woman to fall so badly that she dies, and disappear without leaving a trace of evidence?"

Calderwood shrugged.

"And I can't get a handle on Jordan Lambie either," McCord went on. "According to Pamela Boyd and Aiden Springfield, he's a villain, but Donald Murray seems to think he is just the protective husband, and an hour before her death they're having a nice time in a restaurant and rush home for a romantic evening. So, which is it?"

Calderwood shrugged again. "Perhaps we'll get a breakthrough at Keira Lambie's funeral," he said. "Upshaw might turn up, and you could observe his and Lambie's reaction."

McCord felt slightly less miserable. "Maybe somebody will talk when they see the coffin and face up to the reality that Kiera was brutally killed."

Calderwood's eyes lit up. "I have an even better idea," he said with a mischievous smile. "You should take Amy with you. Lambie doesn't know her, and she can unobtrusively tag along with the Green Fist members. That way we have two sets of eyes and ears there."

"I suppose," McCord said hesitantly.

"What's the problem?" Calderwood asked, although he knew fine well what it was. "Hunting criminals together; surely, it doesn't get more romantic than that?"

McCord sighed. "She's probably still mad at me."

"I doubt it. Even if she hates being patronised, she must see that you had a point and were only concerned about her safety. And," Calderwood added, playing his trump card, "she's never yet turned down an opportunity to be involved in an investigation, has she? I'm sure she'll jump at the chance."

McCord sighed again. "She'll be insufferably smug if I ask her."

"All I'm saying is 'plus one'," Calderwood said. "Go on, give her a call."

With another, even deeper sigh, McCord pressed Amy's speed dial number. She picked up after the third ring.

"Hi, it's me," he said unnecessarily. "I thought you'd like to know that I've had Aiden Springfield in for a chat, and I warned him about Upshaw. Because of what you told us about the roses," he added. "He confirmed they came from him."

"I'm glad." She sounded gratified. "How's the investigation going? You must have come unstuck if you're calling me."

Seeing Calderwood's warning glance, McCord swallowed the response lying on his tongue.

"You're right for once," he said instead. "We're not getting anywhere." He took a deep breath. "Do you fancy coming to Keira Lambie's funeral with me?"

Amy's laughter rang through the office. "Isn't that a little morbid as a venue for a date?"

McCord's face turned crimson.

"It's not a *date*. You won't even be there *with* me; in fact, you'll pretend that we don't know each other. You'll go as a member of The Green Fist who is mourning her friend Keira. Call it undercover, if you like."

"Ah," Amy said, still giggling. "Now you're talking. I'll dig out my little black dress. See you – or rather not see you – there."

She put the phone down.

"Well done," Calderwood said.

McCord was looking for sarcasm in his partner's voice, but Calderwood seemed genuinely pleased.

"Can you believe she thought I was asking her out on a date?" McCord asked, still mortified.

Calderwood grinned. "Since it's the two of you we're talking about, I'd say it is as good as one."

"Rubbish," McCord said grimly. "Let's hope something happens at that funeral to make all this worthwhile."

Which just goes to show that one should be careful what one wishes for.

Chapter 15

The West Lothian Crematorium in Livingston was a modern, rectangular structure set amongst well-kept lawns and young, insubstantial trees. At the front entrance, a pointed wooden roof was supported by four oversized square pillars made of fawn-coloured bricks that gave an impression of immovable solidity. The rear end of the building had probably once been a cottage and seemed to huddle into the ground. Protruding at the back was a chimney, broad but very low as if it was trying to be as inconspicuous as possible.

A part of Amy found this rational and business-like way of disposing of the dead reassuring. The body in the coffin, covered in flowers, would be gently moved and discreetly hidden behind a curtain. Afterwards, it would be returned to the grieving family as ashes, stored tidily in a neatly labelled urn.

And yet, the remnants of her Catholic upbringing missed the brutal honesty of the body being lowered into a hole in the ground and covered with earth; the flesh being left to decay until nothing would remain but bones. She missed the pomp and circumstance with a priest leading the ancient chants and the spicy, resinous smell of incense that accompanied the eternal battle between heaven and hell for the soul of the departed.

When Martin had asked her – in the well-lit, sober office of *Forth Write* magazine – if she really believed in all this mumbo-jumbo as he irreverently called it, she had honestly replied that she didn't, but whenever she stood close to death, a tiny doubt niggled in her subconscious.

She glanced across to McCord, who was sitting across the aisle from her, at the very back, and wondered whether he was thinking about his mother. As they had agreed beforehand, he ignored her; instead, he was surreptitiously surveying the small congregation. Three women and a man were sitting together in the third row, whispering to each other. Amy guessed they worked at the café where Keira had been a waitress. McCord had told her they had all been interviewed by Calderwood but had nothing more to say about Upshaw or Jordan Lambie than they already knew. A few seats along from the little group, a man in a chequered suit sat on his own, his head bowed.

A whispered conversation drew her attention to the entrance. The crematorium officer, a middle-aged man called Alistair Nesbitt, who had been standing at the door welcoming the members of the congregation with a grave nod, was talking to a young man. Amy strained to hear what they were saying but could not make it out. Nesbitt looked as if he had been born in his suit and had a rigorous daily facial routine. In sharp contrast, the young man had the haggard face of a teen prematurely aged by substance abuse, and his cheap suit hung awkwardly on him as if he had never worn such a garment before. When he opened his mouth to speak, the horrendous state of his teeth suggested that even an NHS dentist's bill was beyond his means.

He was very nervous, but Nesbitt said something encouraging and pointed towards the coffin that stood ready for its brief journey. To Amy's surprise, the young man sat down in the front row on the right-hand side, leaving the left free for Jordan Lambie as the chief mourner.

Amy was wondering who the young man might be, when raised voices from the entrance made everybody turn their heads. Jordan Lambie was remonstrating with

Nesbitt, who was holding his hands up in a gesture of appeasement and urging Lambie to keep his voice down.

"What are they doing here?" Lambie snarled.

A gaggle of Green Fist members, including Pamela Boyd, Aiden Springfield and Donald Murray, were attempting to enter the main hall but finding their way blocked by a furious Jordan Lambie. Amy saw that Nesbitt was beginning to perspire. Such a scene at one of his funerals was not something he had been trained for, and he was clearly at a loss what to do.

Pamela Boyd, dressed in a long skirt in subdued colours, gave Nesbitt a rueful smile and was about to speak when Donald Murray unceremoniously pushed her out of the way and addressed Lambie directly.

"We've come to pay our respects to Keira. We all loved her, and I think she would have wanted us to put our differences aside, at least for this one occasion, don't you think, Jordan?"

Lambie's anger evaporated as quickly as it had arisen. He seemed breathless, and his skin was pewter grey. McCord had told Amy about Lambie's heart condition, and she hoped his medication would see him through the most difficult day of his life.

Nodding at Murray, who patted his arm sympathetically, Lambie moved aside and allowed the group to file in. Boyd walked purposefully to the front, directed the other members to the second row and waited for Murray to follow before taking her seat at the aisle with an unobstructed view of the coffin.

It was time to begin. Everybody fell silent as Jordan Lambie, slowly and bent like an old man, moved past to take his lonely place in the first row. Amy felt a profound sadness at a life that had been brutally cut short before it had even begun in earnest and deep sympathy for the man who had to bear such a loss. She was surprised, though, at the small number of mourners. Keira, of course, had been alone in the world before she married Lambie, but where was his family? Their friends?

McCord caught Amy's eye, and she knew what he was thinking; there was no sign of Anthony Upshaw. Surely, he wouldn't dare to show his face here, but he might well be sneaking around outside unless his mother had kept him under lock and key, of course. Amy gave a start as canned music suddenly swelled from the loudspeakers.

An order of service had been left on the seats, and it was obvious that this was not going to be a religious ceremony.

After a whimsical pop song, Nesbitt read a text, no doubt prepared by Jordan Lambie, detailing in an unctuous voice Keira's difficult start in life and, indirectly and without mentioning names, the suffering she had endured before she came to Edinburgh where she found love and a safe haven, until it was brutally snatched away from her yet again. He ended with a long list of Keira's qualities: her kindness, her love of nature and her angelic patience in the face of adversity.

Nesbitt stepped aside, and at the click of a button, a recording of *All of Me* by John Legend brought tears to people's eyes.

Amy wondered who would read the eulogy. Lambie was in no fit state to do it, and, judging by the exchange at the door, he had not invited the members of The Green Fist to speak. The colleagues from the café were dabbing their eyes and wiping their noses; none of them made a move to get up.

After an awkward pause, the young man in the front row stood up and moved towards the microphone. Gripping the piece of paper containing his speech tightly in trembling hands, he lowered his head and began to read from his script.

"My name is Declan Carr, and I've come here today to speak about Keira," he announced, but immediately ground to a halt as he struggled to decipher the second sentence on the crumpled paper.

Amy tensed. This would be torture, for everybody. But then, Declan Carr seemed to come to a decision. He stuffed the paper into his suit pocket and defiantly looked at his audience.

"Me and Keira were mates," he said quietly, as everybody strained to hear what he had to say. "From when we were in the same class at primary school. She were a bit wild but always kind and never hurt nobody. She had dreams; dreams of a life in a nice house with a big garden and a man who'd take care of her." He paused and swallowed. "I always thought I'd be that man. I thought we had all the time in the world, but I was wrong. We were only fifteen, and while I was pissing about with drugs and petty crime, she took up with a guy who had a nice flat and who told her he loved her. But it was all bollocks."

Amy saw Nesbitt's face contort and his hand jerk up in an involuntary gesture of alarm. Jordan Lambie sat motionless, his head bowed as Declan Carr continued, warming to his theme.

"Keira thought he was Prince Charming, and of course, she didn't listen to me 'cause I was just an ugly, useless git. She broke off all contact with her friends, and I thought she simply wanted to leave her old life behind and start over with a guy who could give her everything she wanted. Then someone told me that Upshaw knocked her about, and I went to see her, but she told me to bugger off. I was so stupid, I never twigged that she was too scared of him to speak to anybody. Then I heard that she had moved in with a couple of girls, so I went there, but they told me she'd left. Left where, I asked, and they said they didn't know; nobody knew. Keira had told them she would go to where Upshaw would never find her. And then they told me what he had done – abused her, stalked her, broke into her flat and raped her, and the police had done nothing about it."

Amy risked another glance at McCord whose eyes were fixed on Carr, his lips set in a thin line. Nesbitt squirmed on the sidelines, clearly hoping for the earth to swallow him up, or, preferably, Declan Carr. At the front, Pamela Boyd nodded solemnly her approval that an abuser was being named and shamed. This eulogy was certainly unique.

"I felt sick," Carr continued, raising his voice. "I wanted to kill him, I did! But I was too much of a coward, and too busy finding my next hit. I told myself that she was safe now. She could have been on another planet, as far as I knew, but she was safe. And the only consolation I've got is that she found a man to look after her and a lovely home, at least for a little while."

Carr looked at Lambie, who kept his head down.

Nesbitt dabbed his forehead with a pristine handkerchief, praying that Carr had finished on a conventional note. But no such luck.

"...until that animal hunted her down again, and this time he killed her!" Carr went on, with a hysterical undertone in his voice. "It's my fault. It's all our faults for not looking after her! And he's still a free man. Where is justice for Keira?!" he shouted at the top of his voice. "Where?!"

It was as if the building itself was holding its breath. There was no sound apart from the dry sob coming from the depth of Carr's bony chest and the faint squeak of his cheap trainers as he returned to his seat.

Nesbitt hastily stepped forward, mortified but also relieved that this ignominious chapter in the unblemished history of West Lothian Crematorium was over.

"Please stand in respectful silence as we are saying goodbye to Keira Lambie, safe in the knowledge that she is now at peace and free from earthly worries."

As if by magic, the curtain parted with a low whirring sound that was magnified by the silence but soon lost in the first chords of Vangelis' *La Petite Fille de la Mer* as the coffin glided noiselessly into the dark space behind. The curtains closed immediately as if to block out not only the view but also the thought of what would happen next. Everybody remained seated until the Vangelis melody had finished, and then a warbling organ piece marked the end of the ceremony.

As soon as Jordan Lambie rose, Amy saw McCord make a beeline for Declan Carr, their new witness to Upshaw's depravity. No doubt McCord had picked up on Keira Lambie's age when Upshaw took up with her, and perhaps he was planning to get him for underage sex, just like they nailed Al Capone for tax evasion rather than his capital crimes.

Amy would have liked to speak to Jordan Lambie to give him her condolences, but he was talking to Aiden Springfield, or rather, Springfield was talking to Lambie in a very animated manner. Springfield had his back to her, but Lambie's face was blank as if he was not taking anything in.

An unobstructed September sun was shining through the window front on the right and had turned the hall into a greenhouse. Amy was keen to get outside into the fresh air and perhaps even catch a glimpse of Upshaw lurking behind a bush. McCord had told her to stay close to Lambie, but Springfield was still talking to him. This was more than a few words of condolence, so Amy edged closer until she saw the man in the chequered suit making his way towards her, heading for the exit.

McCord had not mentioned anybody else to look out for, apart from Lambie's sister, who was conspicuous by her absence, so Amy intercepted the man in the chequered suit with the subdued smile appropriate for such an occasion.

He seemed surprised to be accosted by a stranger at a funeral but smiled back. His eyes were red-rimmed, and the corner of a crumpled handkerchief was protruding from his pocket.

"So sad about Keira, isn't it?" Amy said.

The man nodded solemnly. "Tragic. Absolutely tragic. Sean Listerman." He rubbed his right palm on his trousers and held a sticky hand out for Amy to shake. "Sorry. It's like a sauna in here."

Proud of her investigator's nose, she shook his hand. Sean Listerman, the butcher. The one who had withdrawn from the land sale and, indirectly, caused Jordan Lambie's solar panel project to fail.

"Pleased to meet you," she said, entirely sincere. "I'm Simone, a friend of Keira's." She hoped he was not a fan of her articles in *Forth Write* magazine and had seen her picture there. "How did you know her?"

"I'm… an old friend of Jordan's. We were at school together."

Amy was surprised. With his fleshy frame and old-fashioned outfit, he seemed much older.

"How nice," she said.

"School was definitely not nice," Listerman said. "I was the little fat guy and I was bullied a lot. But Jordan was my best pal. He was bullied as well because of his stammer, but he stood up for me despite his weak heart."

"Good for him," Amy said with feeling. "I'm sure he's glad of your support today."

Listerman's face clouded over, and when he said nothing, Amy decided to have a stab in the dark about Lambie's sister. Maybe he was more willing to talk about others than himself.

"I was wondering why Beth isn't here," she said. "I hope she's not unwell?"

Listerman looked at her, nonplussed.

"Beth? I'd have been surprised to see her here. Pleased, of course," he hastily added, "but, I didn't expect her to come, did you?"

"Not really," Amy said, trying to conceal her complete ignorance about anything to do with Beth Lambie, "but still, you'd have thought that she would have come to her sister-in-law's funeral."

"You haven't met her, have you?" Listerman asked.

Amy cringed, but recovered quickly. "No, I haven't, but when I asked Keira once about siblings, she said that she had none herself, but that her husband had a sister."

"I can't imagine Keira being very complimentary about Beth," Listerman said. "Jordan didn't get on with his sister at all. Never. Not even as children."

"What a shame," Amy said. "I'm an only child, and I would have loved a sister or a brother."

Listerman was sympathetic. "Of course, you would. Family is the most important thing. I have two younger brothers and a sister, and we are in and out of each other's houses all the time. Especially now we have the wee ones." He pulled out his wallet and flipped it open. The photo showed Listerman proudly embracing a rosy-cheeked woman with a sleeping baby in her arm and a grinning toddler on her knee.

"They are gorgeous," Amy gushed. "You are a very lucky man."

She wondered how she could bring him back to the topic of the Lambies, when a shout rang out from near the entrance. "A doctor, is there a doctor here?"

Amy and Listerman exchanged a concerned look and rushed towards the door, but they were overtaken by McCord, who zoomed past them and dispersed the group of Keira's former colleagues who were staring at somebody lying on the floor. Following in McCord's wake, Amy saw Jordan Lambie writhing on the carpet clutching his left arm and grinding his teeth in pain. A film of cold sweat was glistening on his forehead.

"Call 999," McCord told Amy. "Suspected heart attack." He knelt down next to Jordan Lambie. "Do you have your meds with you?"

"Took some already," Lambie gasped.

Amy pressed the three numbers and answered the operator's questions, stressing Lambie's serious heart condition. They promised an ambulance would be with them shortly.

Lambie moaned softly, wrapped in his own pain and seemingly unaware of the people crowding around him.

"Give us some space, will you?" McCord barked at them, and everybody took a few steps back apart from Amy who hunched down next to McCord and stroked Lambie's head. "The ambulance will be here soon, Jordan," she said. "Just hang on in there."

She jumped when Lambie suddenly sat up and gripped McCord's arm.

"I loved her," he whispered. He opened his mouth to say more but was seized by a violent convulsion that only lasted a few seconds. After a last, pleading look at McCord, he closed his eyes and became limp.

McCord unbuttoned Lambie's shirt and started resuscitation. Framed by the navy cloth, his chest seemed ghastly white. Amy found herself counting and muttering the song lyrics she had been taught in her first aid course to help with the rhythm of the chest compressions. Ah, ha, ha, ha, staying alive… staying alive… McCord soon began to sweat profusely from his exertions, but Lambie showed no sign of life. After thirty compressions, McCord administered two rescue breaths although he was gasping for air himself. The male café employee stepped closer and tapped on McCord's shoulder, indicating he could take over, which McCord gladly accepted.

Amy went outside to see if the ambulance was on its way. The drive was empty bar a couple of cars which were probably on their way to the next timetabled slot in the crematorium schedule. She could hear no siren in the distance, but from the car park round the corner, the cool breeze carried raised voices across to her.

Curious, Amy hurried to the side of the building where, about twenty yards away, a woman in her fifties was lecturing a man who had his back to Amy. The woman finished her tirade, slung her handbag over her shoulder in a gesture that indicated that this altercation was over, and turned towards her car. After a moment's hesitation, the man grabbed the handbag with both hands, yanked it off the woman's shoulder and hurled it to the ground. The woman, her face stony, squared up to the man and said something to him in a quiet voice. Amy thought she could feel his resentment even across the distance, but he picked up the bag and obediently handed it back to the woman. As slowly as physically possible, he opened the door of the VW Golf next to him and strapped himself in. The woman dusted down her bag, got into the Audi that was parked next to the Golf and drove off. She didn't notice Amy who could only make out a perfectly coiffed head and a hard-set mouth.

Eventually, the Golf started up as well and drove past Amy, who caught a glimpse of the man's furious face. It was Anthony Upshaw.

Chapter 16

Amy ran back inside to tell McCord what she had witnessed but remembered just in time that they were not supposed to be seen together.

McCord had taken over the chest compressions again. She could see from the way his jaw was set that his arms were beginning to hurt. Lambie was lying there, jerking slightly with each thump on his chest, like a rag doll being pummelled.

Nesbitt stood over them, wringing his hands. The very purpose of his profession, nay, his calling, was to deliver a calm, dignified disposal of the dead. He was comfortable dealing with the deceased and their bereaved relatives, but somebody dying on the freshly hoovered purple carpet was an entirely different matter.

Eventually, there was a faint wailing sound that grew rapidly stronger, and Amy ran outside again. The ambulance was speeding up the drive. She waved to the driver, and the vehicle came to an abrupt halt in front of the main entrance.

Two men in green shirts jumped down, opened the rear door and pulled out a stretcher. Amy decided to wait outside, hoping to get some indication of the state Lambie was in when they came back with him.

After less than a minute, the paramedics reappeared, carrying a motionless Lambie on the stretcher with an oxygen mask over his face. With well-rehearsed movements, they smoothly pushed their patient inside the ambulance and closed the double doors with a thud. But the vehicle did not move.

The congregation, curious about the delay, was gathering in the forecourt, and one of the café workers, whose husband had suffered a heart attack, explained with some relish to the blissfully ignorant what was happening. Amy heard the paramedics moving around inside the vehicle, and after what seemed an age, a faint, continuous bleep. Eventually, that stopped, too. A couple of minutes later, the ambulance drove off at a steady pace.

Slowly, Amy followed the small group back into the building texting McCord to let him know that Upshaw had been outside, when two things happened at exactly the same time. From a side door that had been opened to let in some air, an ashen-faced Donald Murray staggered towards McCord, while a blood-curdling scream from outside made everybody freeze. Poor Mr Nesbitt's worst ever day at work was not over yet.

After ascertaining with a fleeting glance that Donald Murray was at least physically unhurt, McCord left the incoherently babbling man in the care of the stunned Nesbitt and rushed out of the side door where Murray and the scream had come from.

A few steps away, one of the café workers stood, shaking. She was staring at the ground and crying hysterically. Lying alongside the wall was Pamela Boyd, the back of her head soaked in blood, her eyes staring ahead, unseeing. A crimson stain on the whitewashed wall indicated that her head had been hit against it with some force.

Fighting off a bout of nausea, McCord pulled out his phone and called for backup and for Dr Crane. After reading Amy's text, he also put out an arrest warrant for Anthony Upshaw.

With a start, he realised Amy had appeared at his side. He tried to shield her from the sight of the corpse, but she had taken in the situation in a flash and threw him a glance that contained everything he needed at this moment; the reassurance that she was fine and that she had every confidence in him. She took the café worker by the arm and gently led her away, muttering soothing clichés.

By now, everybody had appeared at the scene, trying to catch a glimpse of the victim and expressing incredulity at this shocking turn of events.

McCord shut them up with one impatient wave of his hand.

"Please go back into the main hall and wait for my colleagues to arrive. Nobody is to leave this building until we have taken everyone's statement."

* * *

Twenty minutes later, to Nesbitt's immeasurable distress, the remaining funeral slots for that day had been cancelled, and the whole place was crawling with SOCOs.

After securing the crime scene, they were busy gathering evidence and taking photographs.

McCord instructed the local police constables who had responded to his call for backup to take witness statements and DNA samples from everybody present. If anyone refused, they were to be sent straight to him. He wanted an exact account of everybody's whereabouts after the service, including who had been speaking to whom at what time. He also alerted the officers to Amy's presence. She was sitting with the members of The Green Fist, no doubt making her own, covert inquiries. They were to treat her like any other witness and not to blow her cover.

Following McCord's call, Calderwood had dropped everything and made his way to the crematorium, only stopping to pick up a couple of takeaway coffees and bacon rolls because it sounded as if it would be a long session. A coffee in hand and with his loyal and sympathetic partner at his side, McCord snapped out of crisis mode. After recounting the chaotic events, including his futile attempts to keep Jordan Lambie alive, he regained the sense of detachment needed for an effective investigation.

Donald Murray had been led into a separate room and, clutching his second mug of sugary tea, was waiting for McCord. His face was a healthier colour, and he was keen to get on with his statement.

"When they had put Jordan in the ambulance, I went out the side door for a smoke. That's when I found Pamela." He shuddered. "It was like something out of a horror movie."

"Did you touch the body or anything in its vicinity?" McCord asked, while Calderwood took notes.

"Good God, no," Murray said. "As soon as I realised what had happened, I ran to find you. Why were you at the funeral, anyway?"

"It's procedure in unsolved cases," McCord said. "It shows respect for the family. It's also often the case that the killer attends the funeral, and we might be able to make useful observations. Why do you ask?" he added, his eyes narrowing with suspicion.

"I... I just wondered," Murray stammered. "It seemed a little... intrusive."

"By their very nature, murder investigations are intrusive," McCord said. "There is no privacy anymore for those involved. Surely, catching a killer and getting justice for the victim takes precedence?"

"Of course, of course," Murray hastily agreed.

"When you came towards me, you mumbled something that I couldn't make out," McCord said. "What was it you wanted to tell me?"

Murray shrugged. "I don't remember. I think I was in deep shock."

"Understandably," Calderwood remarked, before McCord, who was sceptical, could say anything.

"Why did you put me in a separate room from the others?" Murray asked. "I don't know anything!"

"You found the body," Calderwood said. "You had a particularly nasty shock, and you might have seen something important."

"And," McCord added, happy to rattle Murray a little more, "I don't remember seeing anybody else coming in before you, so the thought had occurred to me–"

"That I...? That's absurd!"

McCord raised his eyebrows.

"So, you were good friends with Pamela Boyd, then?"

"We weren't exactly best pals," Murray replied slowly, kneading his fingers, "but surely you don't think I killed her? Everything happened exactly as I said. I went outside for a smoke and found her lying there. I ran back in to tell you, and that's it."

"Do you have any idea who might have wanted to kill Ms Boyd?" McCord asked.

Murray shook his head. "We're an environmental group, not a bunch of criminals. Pamela and her disciples pulled a few stunts, public order offences and the like, but we don't kill people."

"Did she ever mention being threatened by anybody? An Anthony Upshaw perhaps?"

"She didn't mention anything to me. You mean the Anthony…?"

"The man who Keira Lambie claimed had stalked her, yes."

Murray's eyes widened. "You think he was the burglar who killed Keira? And he came back to kill Pamela?"

"There is no evidence of either," McCord said quickly. "We're exploring different avenues."

Murray gave him a wink.

"You have to say that, don't you? But Keira's old friend, who gave that eulogy, he had no doubts about Upshaw's guilt, did he?"

"Mr Carr hasn't come forward with any new information. He should not have accused Mr Upshaw publicly. If this gets in the papers, he might have landed himself with a libel case and jeopardised any possible future prosecution. I've had a word with him already."

"This Upshaw wasn't here today, though, was he?" Murray asked. He screwed his face up in an effort to remember. "I knew everybody… apart from the tall, bald guy. He was here with a bunch of women," he added excitedly. "The one who helped you resuscitate Jordan."

"That was a former colleague of Mrs Lambie from the café," McCord said. "I must ask you not to speculate about an ongoing case, at least not in public."

But Murray could not resist an attempt to wheedle some information out of the detectives.

"So, you're saying this Upshaw was not here, today. Perhaps he is innocent, then?"

"He was certainly not in the congregation," McCord said. He felt Calderwood glancing at him; he'd had no chance yet to tell him about Amy's message. "Right. If you

have no further information for us, Mr Murray…"
McCord rose to indicate the interview was over.

"I'm sorry I can't help you," Murray said, heaving himself out of the chair. "But if I do hear anything, you'll be the first to know."

"Thank you," McCord said. "Goodbye."

When Murray had closed the door behind him, McCord threw his empty cup in the bin.

"He recovered pretty quickly from his deep shock, didn't he?" he said to Calderwood. "But let's see if we can fast-track Amy's statement. She saw Upshaw outside. I've put a warrant out for his arrest. Gilchrist won't like it, but needs must!"

Chapter 17

Back at St Leonard's, McCord had the unpleasant task of briefing Superintendent Gilchrist about the morning's events. His superior's expression oscillated between horror and despair.

"Only you, Detective Inspector McCord, could go to the funeral of a crime victim whose killer has not yet been apprehended and end up with not one, oh no, with *two* more bodies. Are you collecting them, by any chance?"

McCord had expected this reaction but still bristled at the injustice of it all.

"Jordan Lambie had a congenital heart condition. I can hardly be held responsible for his cardiac arrest," he said sharply.

"Which will still require a post-mortem," Gilchrist pointed out. "A young man of twenty-six; we can't simply ignore that."

"He was at the funeral of his wife," McCord pointed out. "It doesn't get more stressful that that."

"Especially when the investigating officer has insinuated that he might be responsible for her death," Gilchrist said. "Or is he no longer a suspect?"

"I'm keeping an open mind," McCord said.

Gilchrist was pacing up and down his office.

"And where are we with Pamela Boyd's murder? A murder which, I'd like to point out, happened right under your nose. The hacks will be jumping for joy. I could write tomorrow's headlines for them. 'Eco Queen murdered next door to DI'!"

"I was kind of busy trying to keep Jordan Lambie alive," McCord snapped.

"Not very successfully either," Gilchrist said, stopping in his tracks. "And can you explain why you've issued a warrant for Anthony Upshaw's arrest? Again, without consulting me?"

McCord felt on safer ground now.

"He was seen outside the crematorium seconds before Boyd's body was found, which means that for the second time in a fortnight he was in the vicinity of the scene of a violent death. Wouldn't you agree that this is a strange coincidence? We need to get forensics to have a look at his clothes again. If he killed Boyd, he would have blood spatter on them."

"I suppose we'll have to interview him again," Gilchrist conceded, a little deflated. "But we wouldn't be in this position if we had been able to charge him with Keira Lambie's murder. We need something resembling evidence this time, or we'll have a lawsuit for police harassment on our hands. Have you found any connection between Upshaw and Boyd?"

"Not yet, sir," McCord admitted.

"What about the other people at the crematorium? You've just told me that only a dozen or so people attended the service. It can't be that hard to figure out who killed her, surely."

"Anybody could have slipped out while I was resuscitating Lambie," McCord said, "and some had motive, including the man who found her, but–"

"Well, you'd better get on with it then."

And with that, McCord was dismissed.

* * *

McCord and Calderwood were going through the witness statements when Amy turned up at the station.

"We're lucky it was a small funeral," McCord said. "At least there are a limited number of suspects."

"I don't know why you bother," Amy said. "Surely, you should be going after Anthony Upshaw. He was seen in the vicinity of two murder scenes, with two women as victims. Even the injuries are similar. Both Keira Lambie and Boyd ended up with fatal head wounds."

"Point taken," McCord said, "but I think we can assume that it was his mother who was at the crematorium with him, and she will vouch for his innocence."

"She can't, though," Amy said. "They came in separate cars. She must have found out or guessed that he would turn up at the funeral and gone there to keep him out of trouble. What if he was there first and did the deed before she arrived? It would have only taken seconds."

Calderwood sighed. "But we have no witnesses, Amy. Everybody was watching Lambie having a heart attack."

"Everybody apart from Boyd and her killer," McCord corrected him. "The problem is: why would Upshaw want Boyd dead? He probably didn't even know her. We have to consider those who were at the funeral. Any of them could have slipped outside and killed her. What was she doing there anyway?"

"It was hot in the main hall," Amy said. "She probably popped out for a bit of fresh air."

"Maybe she met somebody?" Calderwood thought aloud. "Somebody she wanted to talk to without the others from the group knowing about it?"

"It doesn't look to me as if it was a planned attack," McCord said. "Far too risky with so many people around, and the killer couldn't have known that Lambie would die so conveniently. Also, to bash somebody's head against a wall like that seems more like a crime of passion, although Boyd didn't strike me as somebody with a busy love life. But I could be wrong, of course," he added hastily, seeing the corners of Calderwood's mouth twitch.

"I think you can rule out the people from the café where Keira Lambie worked," Amy said. "Whenever I checked on them, they were all together."

"And they all remember that one of them" – Calderwood rifled through the statements trying to find the name of the woman – "was telling the others what the paramedics were doing in the ambulance. With there being four of them from the café, I think they would have noticed if one of them had gone off."

"Perhaps," McCord said, "but I think it is too early to rule anybody out. Still, as far as we know, there is no connection between the café and The Green Fist apart from Keira Lambie, so I think until we've got Upshaw back in, we should start with the group of activists."

"Yes, I picked up a lot of tension there," Amy said, "but with the funeral going on, nobody said anything explicit. I'm going back there tomorrow to see what the chat is."

"Oh, no, you're not," McCord said. "Murray claims to have found her, but he could easily have killed her."

"It was Upshaw who killed her, I'm sure of it," Amy said. "You concentrate on finding evidence, and I'll find out what was going on in that group if indeed there was anything going on. They won't talk to you because they don't like the police, and they think you suspect them."

"Which I do," McCord said, "until we know otherwise. The group is the only thing that links all three victims."

"Exactly, so let me scout them out. You don't need to worry about me. Murray is just an old lecher. He seriously thinks he can charm every woman he fancies with his innuendo. I'll make sure I'm not alone with him," Amy said. "No, I'm going," she added to silence McCord's protest.

"I think one person we can leave aside is Declan Carr," Calderwood said to deflect Amy and McCord from their squabble. "He has no connection with Keira's new life, and from what he was saying, the only person he might want to kill is Anthony Upshaw."

"Which shows that he is a good judge of character. What did you make of him?" Amy asked McCord. "You talked to him for quite a while after his eulogy."

"Hopeless for the witness stand in any court," McCord said. "Told me himself that he has a rap sheet as long as Leith Walk. I believe he genuinely cared for Keira, and he is convinced that Keira's accusations against Upshaw were the truth, and that he killed her. But he has no proof of anything, and him holding a torch for her doesn't help his credibility either."

"She must have been quite a woman," Amy said with a wistful look. "Keira, I mean. She was only nineteen and had three men who adored her."

McCord tilted his head in disbelief. "Yes – a junkie, a Billy No-Mates and a complete nutter who by all accounts stalked and killed her. You're not jealous of her, are you?"

"Of course not, I just meant… ach, never mind. What about the butcher?"

"What butcher?" Calderwood asked.

"Sean Listerman," McCord said. "Old school friend of Jordan Lambie. He was there on his own, so nobody would have noticed him slipping out, but surely he was more interested in what was happening to his friend than murdering a green activist."

"He and Lambie were not all that friendly, though," Amy said. "It was the way Listerman talked about him. And they weren't sitting together either. Of course, Listerman was supposed to sell his land to Lambie for his solar farm and then withdrew. Lambie must have been furious."

"Fascinating," McCord said insincerely, "but immaterial now that Lambie is dead. I'm afraid, there's nothing for it. We need to wait for the PM on Boyd. Crane said he would try to squeeze it in tomorrow and, hopefully, forensics will find something conclusive on the crime scene or in Boyd's phone records and emails. But first, we'll need to hear what Mr Upshaw, or rather his mother, has to say."

* * *

To avoid further events contributing to his latent stomach ulcer, Gilchrist had insisted on conducting the interview with Upshaw himself, aided by Calderwood, who understood the delicate nature of the situation. McCord had been relegated to the video link next door where he would be able to observe how things were done properly.

McCord settled into the upholstered chair, looking forward to the uneven battle between Gilchrist and stony-faced Patricia Upshaw, who had her resentful son in tow.

Greeted by a small bow and inviting hand gesture from Gilchrist, Patricia Upshaw lowered herself gingerly onto the plastic chair as if it might bite, and placed her leather briefcase on the table to remind them of her status as a legal representative. She began by complaining bitterly about the indignity of having to bring her son again into an interview room as if he was a common criminal.

She was right, thought McCord, common he was not; as far as he was concerned, Upshaw was much worse.

"My dear Mrs Upshaw, you will understand that Mr Upshaw's sighting at the scene of a murder left us no choice but to include him in our investigation," Gilchrist said as if an apology was needed, "even if it is only to eliminate him as a suspect as quickly as possible."

"Who claims to have seen my son at the scene of the murder?" Patricia Upshaw demanded.

McCord broke out in a sweat. "Please don't mention Amy, you moron," he muttered.

"A very reliable witness saw you and Mr Upshaw straight after the murder in the car park," Gilchrist replied.

McCord wiped his brow.

Patricia Upshaw sighed theatrically. "Ah, here we go again. Sloppy investigating and then jumping to premature conclusions. You're right, Superintendent, this will be quick. What you are, in fact, saying is that my son and I were seen not at the scene of the murder but somewhere in the vicinity, the emphasis being on my *son and I*, and I don't believe you are deluded enough to believe that together we killed a woman neither of us has ever met before. Your... unusual detective inspector might be, but I see that you had the sense to take him off the investigation."

"DI McCord hasn't been taken off the investigation," Gilchrist corrected her, and McCord noticed the note of regret in his voice. "But the fact remains that your son – theoretically, of course – could have committed the murder before you arrived. You were observed driving away in separate cars," he added. "Given Mr Upshaw's... history, I had no choice but to bring him in for questioning."

"Are you going to ask him any questions, then?" McCord blurted out, "or are you just going to kowtow to his bleeding mother?" He quickly checked that the setting of the microphone was only one way, which to his relief it was.

"There is no 'history'," Mrs Upshaw was saying. "I thought we had established that at our last meeting. My son felt he should pay his respects to his former girlfriend, as any decent man would do. I had strongly advised him not to, and I think he realises now that he should have taken my advice. Because clearly, your department is determined to punish my son for crimes he did not commit."

"Nothing could be further from our minds," Gilchrist said, with urgency, "but we… I must be seen to follow each avenue of the investigation, however far-fetched it might seem."

"Far-fetched? Aye, right," McCord said out loud, his leg bouncing up and down with frustration.

"Well, I expect your forensics people to have left by the end of today, and as they are not going to find anything, I'll assume that this matter is finished."

Picking up her briefcase, she rose and waved to her son to do the same.

"One moment, please," Calderwood said. "Since we might not have the opportunity to speak to you again, may I ask a question that has been bothering me?"

McCord had no idea what Calderwood was doing. Patricia Upshaw set her leather briefcase back on the table with an irritated thud; her son remained in his seat, impassive, but Gilchrist tensed and frowned at his protégé.

"I'm sure you can put my mind at rest in a second," Calderwood said with his disarming smile. "If Mr Upshaw is innocent of all the accusations made against him by Keira Lambie, why did you feel you had to pay her one thousand pounds?"

McCord punched the air. "Good man, Calderwood!" he shouted at the monitor.

Patricia Upshaw froze.

Her son turned his face to her, realisation slowly dawning. Then he jumped up. "It was you! You drove her away. It's all your fault!"

He moved towards her, his face white, his hands clenched into fists.

A panic-stricken Gilchrist raised his hands. "Mr Upshaw, please, calm down. I'm sure this is all a misunderstanding."

Patricia Upshaw, her jaws set, held her son's eyes until his arms dropped by his side and his strong frame seemed to shrink.

Then she turned on Calderwood.

"Did you have a warrant to access my accounts?" she asked him, belligerently.

"No," Calderwood said as Gilchrist blanched, "but we had a warrant to access Mrs Lambie's account, and one of our officers, who has excellent IT skills, was able to trace the payment back to you even though you went to considerable lengths to send the sum anonymously."

"Yes," McCord urged his partner on. "Go, get her!"

Patricia Upshaw only needed a second to process this.

"That girl's lies would not have got her anywhere; they would certainly never have made it to court, so a lengthy investigation was not in anybody's interest, not in my son's and not in hers, either. I thought giving her the opportunity to withdraw with some dignity and make a fresh start was the most sensible course of action. And thankfully, acts of kindness are not illegal yet."

"Dignity? Kindness?" McCord spat. "Bitch!"

He stopped himself as Gilchrist shot an angry glance at the camera. It took McCord a moment to reassure himself that Gilchrist could neither see nor hear him, but he certainly suspected that McCord was behind this ambush. But then Gilchrist addressed Patricia Upshaw again. "Thank you for clearing that up for us, Mrs Upshaw. Please come this way."

Gilchrist and the Upshaws filed out as Calderwood stopped and saved the recording. Then he looked up and winked at the camera.

Chapter 18

The following morning, a leaden sky lay heavy over the city, and on her journey to Currie, Amy had turned the car's heating on high.

To her great disappointment, she found that the sign on the door of the zero-waste shop had been turned to 'closed'. This was not surprising under the circumstances; even though Murray would not be beside himself with grief over the loss of Pamela Boyd, etiquette demanded that a certain amount of respect was shown to the recently deceased, especially when they had been murdered.

The lights were on, however, and Amy was not ready to give up just yet. Surreptitiously, she peeked through the window to assess the situation. In the middle of the shop, Donald Murray and Aiden Springfield were engaged in a heated conversation. Amy turned her back to the window and edged closer, pretending to check something on her phone. She could make out muffled voices from within that became louder and, eventually, distinguishable. Amy thanked a higher power that Donald Murray had not had the funds to install triple glazing.

"I swear on my daughter's life, I didn't kill Pamela, so stop your nonsense!" Murray was shouting.

Then everything went quiet. Amy turned round and saw Springfield slumped on a chair, his shoulders shaking. Murray was patting him on the shoulder when his eyes caught Amy standing outside.

Reminding herself of her undercover persona, she gave him a little wave and made a gesture asking if she could come in. Murray turned the key and, accompanied by the incongruously cheerful jingle of the door, Amy entered the shop.

"I'm sorry to interrupt," she said towards Springfield, who was wiping his face on the sleeve of his sweatshirt. "I wondered if I could be of any help."

"Hi, Simone," Murray said, far less jovial than before. Amy wondered if he suspected her of eavesdropping on them. "We're closed today, but perhaps you can persuade Aiden that being beaten by Pamela in a leadership contest is not sufficient motive for killing her."

"Of course, it isn't," Amy said as forcefully as she could.

"I'm sorry." Springfield sniffed. "It's all been too much."

Murray patted the young man's shoulder again.

"He's taken Keira's death very badly," he said quietly to Amy as if Springfield had suddenly gone deaf. "And now poor Pamela as well… I'll make us some coffee. Sit yourself down. We could do with some cheering up."

"Who could do such a thing?" Springfield said with a thick voice. "Pamela was such a great woman; she was an inspiration, not just to me, but many. This journalist, Whatshisname, might have uncovered the illegality of the project, but it was Pamela who persuaded Listerman to withdraw from the land sale, and without that, the project was dead. Nobody contributed more to the cause than her."

"And Keira never got involved in the fight against her husband's project?" Amy asked.

Springfield shook his head. "It just shows what a great friend Pamela was to Keira. Despite their political differences, she told Keira over and over again to take the fight to Upshaw and to her husband, but Keira wouldn't.

It made me sick how he pretended to grieve when it was his fault that she was dead."

"You didn't say that to the poor man at the funeral?" Amy burst out.

Springfield's eyes were watery, but defiant. "Poor man? The brute imprisoned her and didn't even keep her safe. If she'd come away with me, she would have been free and happy…"

He started to cry again.

Murray shook his head. "I think we should try to remember Keira and Pamela as they were," he said. "Shall we show Simone the video of the demonstration?" he said to Springfield like a father trying to distract his child. "She never met Keira at her glorious best."

Springfield nodded, and Murray began searching for it on his phone. "Here it is. Somebody recorded the incident, and it even made the news. Tell Simone what happened."

"Me and Keira and Pamela and a few of the others joined the 'Stop the Oil' protest in June," Springfield said, interspersed with hiccups.

"Against my advice," Murray butted in. "Just saying."

"Pamela had persuaded Keira to go along," Springfield continued, more fluent now, "although direct action was not her thing, and I went as well…"

"Because of Keira," Murray finished the sentence for him. "I'd told you this was not your scene, but nobody listens to me anymore."

"It turned quite ugly," Springfield continued, ignoring Murray's comment, and pointed to the row of riot police with their protective shields and helmets slowly advancing with a frightening inevitability like an army of giant insects. "We had stopped all the traffic on the ring road, and some of us were throwing things at the police, so they started to arrest people. Here, that's me."

Amy could see a terrified Springfield being collared by a man at least a foot taller and twice his width.

"I thought I was going to die," Springfield said. "He was dragging me towards a police van, and I saw myself locked in a cell forever and going mad…"

Murray smiled. "I don't think it would have been that bad, son," he said. "The way Pamela talked about the times she had been arrested, I'm sure she thoroughly enjoyed herself."

"Because she was fearless," Springfield went on, "and famous. They wouldn't have dared hurt her. But look, there's Keira!"

Amy saw her, looking tiny and very young in a cotton blouse and skinny jeans, squaring up to the policeman and remonstrating with him.

"Let him go," she shouted over the din of the battle and pulled on the policeman's arm. "He hasn't done anything!"

It was impossible to hear what else she said but, for a moment, her determined face filled the screen.

"That must have been how Upshaw found her!" Amy exclaimed.

Murray nodded. "Yes, Keira said that herself. After she had been so careful to keep a low profile, she was caught on television. Tragic."

The camera's focus was now back on the policeman who, aware of being filmed wrestling with an unarmed, cowering man and a young woman half his size, let go of Springfield and motioned them to get out of the melee. The video stopped abruptly, and there was a moment of silence.

"See, and that's why I wanted Keira to be our next leader," Murray said eventually. "She had grit but a great way of dealing with things; by talking, compromise, common sense and, above all, by loving nature and people more than her own ego, unlike others." He waved Springfield's weak protest away. "I know one shouldn't speak ill of the dead. But it's true. After Pamela took over, it was all about Pamela. For Keira, it was about making the world a better place, and our members loved her for that. I'm sure she would have won the next leadership election. Now I'm not sure who is going to take over."

"I don't care about the bloody leadership election!" Springfield shouted. "Without Keira and Pamela, there is no point!"

He jumped up, toppling his chair in the process, and stormed out.

Murray sighed. "The poor boy. The group was like his family. I do hope he comes back when he's had some time to grieve. But here, Simone, we were only talking about ourselves. What do you make of it all? You were at the funeral as well. Who do you think killed Pamela?"

Amy swallowed, conscious of now being on her own with Murray. "I think it was Upshaw. He killed Keira, and he was at the crematorium around the time of Pamela's murder."

Murray nodded. "The most sensible thing I've heard for a week. Currie is not the kind of place where two lunatics go running around murdering people. One is quite enough, I think. I'm making another coffee, would you like one?"

Amy suddenly noticed that there were no cars on the road outside. The pavement was deserted. It was eerily quiet for mid-morning; the only sound came from the raindrops hitting the windowpane and running down like tears over a cold, immoveable face.

"I need to be off," Amy said, hastily grabbing her handbag. "I've just remembered that I have an appointment at half eleven."

"What a pity," Murray said, rising with her to help her quite unnecessarily into her coat. "Now, don't be a stranger, do you hear?"

Amy managed a smile and made for the door. Outside, she took a deep breath. The rain was getting heavier, and the greyness enveloped her like a suffocating blanket. Hunched up, she hurried towards the car.

* * *

"Boring," was Crane's verdict as he covered Pamela Boyd's body with a freshly laundered sheet. "Blunt force trauma to the skull. In other words: somebody grabbed her by the neck and banged her head against the wall. And not only once, but several times with considerable force."

"Could a woman have done it?"

"No doubt about that." The pathologist grinned. "We all know about a woman's wrath, don't we, DI McCord?"

McCord wondered briefly how Crane would have heard about Amy's frequent exasperation with him, but then ignored the pathologist's remark, accepting it as a general observation about the battle of the sexes.

"The good news for you is," Crane continued, "that we found foreign DNA on her neck. The lab guys are running tests on her clothing, too."

"Sweat?" McCord asked, brightening up.

"Unless the killer spat on their hands beforehand to give them a better grip, which is possible but unlikely, wouldn't you say?"

McCord was growing tired of the sarcasm he had been subjected to all day. "You never know, Dr Crane," he said, measuring in his mind the circumference of Crane's incongruously thick neck. "But to be sure, I could always re-enact the crime with you standing in for the victim."

Crane cackled. "And without me doing the PM, you'd probably even get away with murder."

* * *

"Great news, Calderwood," McCord said as he returned to his office with two americanos and muffins from the café across the road. "Boyd's killer left a DNA sample behind. We can compare it to all the samples that were taken from the attendees at the funeral, and if it's none of them, it must be Upshaw. Either way, we've got our killer. And for once, Gilchrist won't have anything to moan about."

"Thanks," Calderwood said, appreciatively taking a sip of his coffee. "I do hope it turns out to be Upshaw. Then, even if we can't prove he killed Keira Lambie, he'll at least go down for this murder. And," he added with a mischievous grin, "you can thank Amy for that because without her, we wouldn't have known he was at the crematorium."

"Have you heard from her at all?" McCord asked, hoping it sounded casual.

"No," Calderwood said. "She's probably still on her way back from Currie. There's roadworks on the Lanark Road. The traffic around there will be torture."

McCord groaned. "Speaking of torture, I must get down to writing that bloody speech. Why the hell do people get married these days anyway? All the best people are living in sin," he said. "I hope you and Dharwan haven't fixed a date yet. I don't think I could cope with another wedding in the next two years."

Calderwood shook his head. "I don't believe I'm hearing this. You practically ordered me to propose to her!"

"That was a totally different situation," McCord said. "And I don't remember you putting up much of a fight."

"Anyway, how do you know you're going to be invited?" Calderwood said. "Judging by the body count at family occasions you've recently attended, it's definitely safer for everybody if you stay away."

There was a perfunctory knock on the door, and Amy entered.

Relieved to see her safely back, McCord pushed his still untouched muffin towards her. "How did you get on?"

"It was very illuminating," Amy said, nodding her thanks. She broke the muffin in two pieces and gave McCord the bigger one back.

"When I arrived, Springfield was accusing Murray of murdering Boyd over the leadership of the group."

"Would he even have a chance?" Calderwood asked. "He was voted out the last time, wasn't he?"

"Murray was pushing for Keira to replace Boyd," Amy said. "And I can see why. Keira wasn't quite the delicate little flower we thought she was." She told them about the video. "But now that Keira is dead, Murray fancies himself as the new leader."

"Interesting that you're not the only one who suspects Murray," Calderwood said to McCord.

"He certainly hated Boyd," Amy said. "He even slagged her off today; the day after she was murdered."

"But would he make it so obvious if he had killed her?" Calderwood asked.

McCord shifted in his seat. The petty squabbles of the tree huggers weren't getting them anywhere.

"There's no point in speculating," he said. "Tomorrow, the DNA on Boyd's body will tell us who killed her."

"What?" Amy exclaimed, but then disappointment spread across her face. "Looks like I've been wasting my time in Currie. Why didn't you tell me straightaway?"

Calderwood gave McCord a meaningful look.

"It's always useful to get some background," McCord said, pretending not to notice. "Did Springfield mention Upshaw at all? I don't like the idea of the two of them meeting in a dark alley."

Amy regarded McCord with surprised satisfaction.

"No, he didn't, but remember I told you that he talked to Jordan Lambie for quite a while at the funeral? Turns out, Springfield didn't make his condolences at all. Instead, he told Jordan what a wonderful friend Boyd had been to Keira and then gave the poor man a piece of his mind! What was he thinking?"

"He was in love," McCord said. "He was not of sound mind."

Calderwood shot a side glance at Amy and laughed.

"You talk about love as if it's a mental illness."

"Maybe not as such," McCord conceded. "But it comes close."

The mention of love reminded him of the unfathomable mystery that was marriage.

"What I don't get," he said, "is why Keira Lambie was so chummy with a woman who was hellbent to scupper her husband's pet project."

"It seems to me that Keira saw Boyd not so much as a friend on equal terms, but more like a guru who supported and guided her. Still, both Springfield and Murray think that Keira never did anything to actively undermine Jordan's project. Anyway," Amy said, getting up to leave, "after spending a whole morning investigating your cases for you, I think I should at least show face at my regular place of work. Phone me as soon as you have the DNA results, and then get Upshaw behind bars!"

* * *

Amy summoned all her self-discipline to concentrate on her article about stalkers, but Martin had other ideas.

"And what are you going to wear to the wedding?" he asked Amy after hovering around her desk for ten minutes.

"Mum's really busy just now with her autumn collection," she said, "so I haven't asked her to make a dress especially for the wedding. Remember the pink dress I wore to the charity ball? That will do."

She remembered McCord failing to find the words to compliment her on it but, on reflection, she was unsure whether he had been stunned or appalled.

"That will do?" Martin echoed disapprovingly. "No, it will not do! You are going there as DI McCord's plus-one, and this is your attitude? This momentous occasion requires planning, preparation and meticulous execution!"

"I think that's exactly how McCord feels about it – an execution," Amy said. "I bet it's all his dad's doing. Now that he's tying the knot, he'll be keen to see his son settled as well."

"And the man is right," Martin said. "So, let's think this through. Is it going to be a formal dance or a ceilidh?"

"What difference does that make?" Amy asked.

"What difference does it make?" Martin appealed to the heavens. "It makes all the difference in the world! If it's a sedate, dignified occasion, your pink dress is suitably ethereal and romantic but you can't possibly wear the same outfit again."

Amy was about to protest, but he silenced her with an imperious gesture of his right arm. "If it's a ceilidh, you need to be dressed for battle. Ceilidhs bring out the worst, or best, in men, depending on how you look at it. Some think they can show off their sexual prowess by hurling their dance partners around like missiles; I've had the bruises to prove it!"

He exposed a thin arm delineating a bruise that was no longer visible.

"You'll be swirling about, so you need a dress that shows off your legs without giving them too much to look at, and when it comes to Strip the Willow, or even before, you'll be taking your shoes off, so think what you're going to look like barefoot."

"I've been to a ceilidh before, you know," Amy said. "And I doubt McCord would tolerate an assault on me. But you do have a point." Mentally, she went through her extensive wardrobe. "Hm. I'm thinking a plain, tight-fitting top and my tartan mini skirt with some accessories?"

Martin was aghast.

"Good God. Far too casual. I'm going to have a word with your mum. A fashion show in Paris is all very well, but there are more important things in life."

"The way she's been talking about McCord, she'll be stitching me into a bin bag," Amy said. "Have you thought of that?"

"She's only worried about her little girl. I'm going to make her see that she can't stand in the way of fate any longer."

"I'm begging you, Martin, stay out of this," Amy pleaded. "It'll only turn into a catfight, and in the end, I'll do what I want anyway."

"That's exactly the problem. You two on your own are hopeless. You need to take a wing man with you–"

"Don't even think about it," said Amy. "You're not invited; and just as well because you are capable of locking McCord and me into a cupboard. You'll simply have to let us get on with it."

Martin heaved a sigh from deep within his bony chest.

"Oh, how I wish you would!"

Chapter 19

"No way!" McCord almost dropped the receiver of the office phone. "Are you sure?"

"One hundred per cent," Fred Foster, the forensic lab assistant, said with a strong emphasis on 'hundred'. "None of the samples you provided is a match to the DNA found on Pamela Boyd's body and clothes."

"It must be Anthony Upshaw's then," McCord said more to himself than the caller.

"Not his either," Foster said.

McCord suspected that the man was enjoying tormenting him.

"However, after I couldn't find a match, I ran it through the national database and I got a hit."

"For God's sake, man," exclaimed McCord. "Who?"

"A Jordan Lambie."

For a brief moment, McCord was speechless.

"It can't be!"

"But it is," Foster insisted, and McCord thought he detected more than a trace of impertinence in his voice. The cheek, when the guy didn't have a clue about the case.

"Jordan Lambie was busy dying of a heart attack when Boyd was murdered!" McCord said. "You must have got something mixed up."

"I double-checked," Foster said, now seriously offended. "No mistake."

McCord's mind raced. "But… I was there when Lambie died; I saw it with my own eyes! How…?"

"It is possible, of course, that the DNA was transferred before the murder," Foster said, more conciliatory now. "Maybe he and the victim had a snog before…?"

"Not likely," McCord said gruffly and sank into deep thought.

Eventually, he heard a puzzled voice. "DI McCord? Are you still there?"

"Yes," McCord said. "Go over Lambie's clothes with a fine-tooth comb; and before you ask, I don't know what we're looking for. Anything at all. ASAP. Bye."

He put the receiver down.

"What was that all about?" Calderwood asked.

"You're not going to believe this. We have only one match for the DNA found on Pamela Boyd and it's Jordan Lambie's."

"That's impossible!"

"That's what I said. But the lab assistant swears blind that it's true. What the hell is going on here, Calderwood?" He stopped as a thought occurred to him. "Hang on."

He picked up his mobile and pressed a speed dial button. When the call was answered, he switched on the loudspeaker.

"Amy? Hi. Do you remember the altercation between Jordan Lambie and The Green Fist guys when he tried to keep them away from the funeral?"

"Of course," Amy's cheerful voice rang out through the office. "Why?"

"Did Lambie touch Boyd at any time then?"

There was a brief pause.

"No, I thought for a moment he might get physical, but all he did was tell the cremation officer to throw them out. You were there, so why are you asking?"

"Lambie's DNA was found on Boyd."

"Lambie's?" Amy sounded both incredulous and dismayed. "Not Upshaw's?"

"Nope. Lambie must have got his DNA on Boyd before the murder. The lab assistant even suggested Lambie and Boyd having a snog. Ridiculous. She could have been his mother."

"You never know," Amy said, mulling over this new angle. "It happens. They could have had an affair and kept it a secret. Lambie wouldn't have wanted his wife to know, and it would have been a major embarrassment to Boyd if the group had found out she was having an affair with her political enemy."

"We'll check her phone records for messages from Lambie. They must have communicated somehow," Calderwood said.

"I hope you're not letting Upshaw off because of this?" Amy said. "He was there! And he didn't only kill Boyd; he stalked, raped and killed Keira Lambie as well, remember?"

"I do remember," McCord said irritably, "but you seem to have forgotten that we have no evidence for any of this."

"I don't care," Amy said. "He's not going to get away with this."

"Amy, don't you–"

But the line had gone dead.

McCord banged his fist on the desk. "The silly woman is going after him, Calderwood, I know it. And what if…"

The office phone rang again.

"McCord!" he barked.

"It sounds as if you're not enjoying your job today," Crane's voice boomed down the line. "Mine, on the other hand, has suddenly become a lot more interesting."

"Why?" McCord asked suspiciously.

"I've just had a wee look-see around the insides of our friend Jordan Lambie."

"And? We know he died of a heart attack."

"The cause of death was indeed cardiac arrest," Crane said, "and he had a serious congenital heart condition, but it was well under control, says his GP. So, I ran a blood test, and guess what?"

McCord found those games very tiresome, and he made no effort to hide his feelings. "What?"

"Lambie had not been taking his calcium-channel blockers for a while."

McCord frowned. "But before he collapsed, Lambie told me he had taken them."

"Well, he hadn't," Crane said.

"Why on earth would he lie about that?" McCord asked.

"I'm a pathologist, not a psychologist," Crane said. "I called Lambie's GP, and he says that Lambie was very meticulous about his meds. For people with a lifelong condition, taking their pills becomes automatic. I'm still running a few tests, and I've sent his pills for analysis, but I thought you should know."

McCord groaned. "What do you think it was then? Suicide? Murder?"

"Finding that out is your job, not mine." Crane chuckled. "Enjoy."

Chapter 20

The following morning, McCord was doing his rounds in the open-plan office, expending some of his nervous energy. It was only one week until the wedding, and he had spent the previous evening flinging crunched-up notes of his non-existent speech into the waste-paper bin. In comparison, dealing with three unsolved murders was a delight.

From the other end of the room, McCord saw Calderwood waving to him miming a phone call, so he sprinted back to his office. It was the forensics lab.

"What have you got?" McCord asked breathlessly.

"We found traces of Pamela Boyd's blood on Jordan Lambie's shirt," the lab assistant said. "And, before you ask, yes, I'm sure. The blood spatter is consistent with him pushing her against the wall and getting tiny droplets on his sleeves and the shoulders. I'll send the full report through by the end of today, but I thought you'd want to know."

McCord was silent as he digested the news.

"You're welcome," the lab assistant said tersely and hung up.

McCord dropped his face on his palms and shook his head. Calderwood watched his boss with concern. "What did he say?"

McCord rubbed his face as if to erase his embarrassment.

"It was Lambie who killed Boyd. What an idiot I've been! I assumed the murder happened while everybody was watching Lambie being given CPR, but he must have snuck out before and killed Boyd."

"But why would he?" Calderwood asked. "Revenge for campaigning against his project? It seems a bit extreme. And why now at his wife's funeral? The scandal broke more than a week ago; would he not have gone for Boyd then?"

"Also," McCord said, "it was Martin, with a little help from Amy, who uncovered the illegal land sale and made it all public. We must ask him if he was threatened by Lambie at any point."

"I'm sure Amy would have mentioned it," Calderwood said.

McCord looked puzzled.

"And there's another thing. This wasn't a planned attack. Boyd and her tree hugger friends came uninvited, and Lambie wanted to throw them out; he only gave in after Donald Murray spoke to him."

"Ironic, isn't it?" Calderwood said. "If Boyd had respected Lambie's wishes, she would still be alive."

"Something must have happened after the service that upset Lambie to the point of making him a killer. Go through the witness statements again. We only concentrated on who could have slipped outside unnoticed after Lambie had collapsed. Amy said he spoke to Springfield but find out who else; and I'll get Sutton to check his phone to see if he got any messages during that time."

Calderwood, however, made no move to start with the witness statements. He merely stared into space.

"What?" McCord asked.

Slowly, Calderwood focused on his boss again. "I've had a terrible thought. If Lambie was capable of killing Boyd, he might well have killed Keira as well."

"So, we're back to the husband," McCord said. "That had been my very first instinct. But, again, why? They were in the middle of a romantic evening – why would he kill her?"

"Maybe Keira found out about his affair with Boyd? And they had a fight that turned violent?"

"Could be," McCord said. "Remember the waitress, Jackie Reeves?"

Calderwood grinned.

"Oh, yes, your latest conquest. She was well up for it. Did you ever get in touch with her again?"

"Haha," McCord said with a shudder, "very funny. She claimed that the Lambies were in an intense conversation, with Jordan doing most of the talking as if trying to win Keira round. What if he denied the affair with Boyd then, but Keira found out later in the evening that it was true?"

McCord forced his mind back to Jordan Lambie's final minutes. "His last words were: 'I loved her'. I assumed he meant his wife, but what if he was talking about Boyd?"

McCord massaged his temples where a headache was beginning to form. For the first time, he wished Amy had been there with her effortless interpretations of human relationships.

"There's another thing I don't get," Calderwood said. "Keira Lambie was offline for a whole day before she died. These days that simply doesn't happen. Nineteen-year-olds are inseparable from their phones. They don't misplace them because they are physically attached to them. They even take them to the toilet."

"Seriously?" McCord said with faint disgust. "But you're right. Get onto the service provider and trace Keira's phone. See if they were working on a phone mast or if there was no reception for any other reason."

"I'm on it. By the way, how are you getting on with your sp–"

"Don't even mention the word," McCord said and went back to the case files to look for the crucial detail they had missed.

* * *

Amy was sitting at her desk in the office of *Forth Write* magazine, absent-mindedly chewing on a pencil. McCord had just been on the phone to tell her that it was Jordan Lambie who had killed Pamela Boyd and that his death was suspicious; he had also urged her again to stay away from Upshaw until they had a clearer picture of what was going on.

She was pleased and annoyed in equal measure by this call; pleased that McCord had for once kept her informed without her badgering him, but annoyed that he kept telling her how to do her job, which was, as she saw it, keeping tabs on criminals that might otherwise evade justice. Martin had gone on and on about how wonderful McCord was and how she should heed his advice, so in order to get some peace, she had sent him to make her a latte. The complexities of the state-of-the-art coffee machine would buy her a few minutes' thinking time.

The discovery of Jordan Lambie's DNA bothered her more than she had admitted to McCord or Martin because it had sown doubt in her mind about Upshaw's guilt. She had been sure that he had killed Pamela Boyd, and now, for the first time, she contemplated the possibility that he was not to blame for Keira's death; at least not directly. She had seen genuine grief in his face when he passed her on Caulderhame Road, and his anger had been directed not at Keira but at the people around her, especially Aiden Springfield if Upshaw had suspected that the roses had come from him.

Was it possible that Keira had made up the stories about him stalking her? She had seemed a genuine person when Amy met her at the shop. Perhaps she had been deluded, rather than been lying? And maybe Jordan had tried to keep her at home because of her mental health issues?

"Thanks," Amy said absent-mindedly when Martin placed a beautiful latte and a hobnob in front of her. She contemplated the distinct layers of the drink and wondered if things weren't as black and white as she had assumed.

"Please tell me you're not hatching a plan to sneak up on Anthony Upshaw and frighten him into a confession," Martin said, pulling up a chair. "Because if you are, I'll tell John and follow you around until you give up this crazy notion or until he has organised a bodyguard."

Amy took a careful sip from her latte, causing the layers to merge. "Actually, I'm beginning to wonder if he is the villain we all think he is."

Martin raised his thin, jet-black eyebrows. "Where is all this coming from?"

"Everybody at The Green Fist believed what Keira Lambie told them, and we believed what everybody told us," Amy said. "Perhaps McCord and his team haven't found any evidence because there is none to find."

"But what about the neighbours?" Martin asked. "They saw him hanging around."

"True," Amy conceded, "but they are the types who suspect every young man in a hoodie of a being a criminal."

She threw her pencil on the desk. "Ach, I don't know. I can't shake off the feeling that Springfield somehow holds the key to this case. Not that he is a suspect, but he's the only person who was close to Keira and who is still alive. I must speak to him myself; he might be more open with me than with the police."

"That sounds like a good plan," Martin said. "But be careful, my darling, only meet him in public places and don't wander off on your own afterwards. Your mum is always beside herself with worry. And so am I."

Amy gave him a kiss on his rouged cheek.

"The less she knows, the better," Amy said, "and the same goes for John, do you hear?"

With a pained face, Martin made a gesture of zipping his mouth shut and returned to his desk.

* * *

It was Crane on the phone.

"Greetings, DI McCord. I hear from our friend at the lab that the dead man was the killer." He chuckled. "It's those cases that make all the tedium worthwhile. But I don't want you to go back to the humdrum life you're leading. I've got something exciting for you."

"You're such a tease," McCord said wearily. "Care to share?"

"I found high levels of ibuprofen in Jordan Lambie's peripheral blood, the liver and gastric contents."

McCord sat up. "I take it that's not good for somebody with his heart condition?" McCord asked.

"Not good at all. Fatal even. And guess what was in Lambie's medicine bottle?"

"Ibuprofen?" McCord ventured.

"We'll make a detective of you yet," Crane said.

"Could it have been a simple mistake?" McCord asked, knowing that he was grasping at straws.

"Only in so far as Lambie didn't realise what he was taking," Crane said. "Some ibuprofen pills from a strip look very similar to the calcium-channel blockers he was prescribed. Congratulations, DI McCord: your dead murderer was murdered." The pathologist sighed with pleasure. "I just love this one. It's becoming more and more like an Agatha Christie whodunnit."

* * *

McCord was standing next to the new incident board that had been set up between Keira Lambie's and Pamela Boyd's, which had Jordan Lambie at its centre.

The team's initial delight at the news that the Boyd case was solved had been replaced by mild despair about the new murder that had landed at their feet while Keira Lambie's death was still unexplained. The bets had been running roughly equally between the husband and the stalker, but now with Lambie as Boyd's killer, the odds had risen considerably in his favour.

"Right," McCord said when the muted conversations had stopped. "Somebody swapped Jordan Lambie's meds. Who had motive and opportunity?"

He pointed to the picture of a square-jawed woman with mousy brown hair cut in a bob.

"Jordan's older sister Beth. She stands to inherit her brother's estate; the house and the shares in Northern Power Energy which might have dropped in value after the land sale scandal, but the inheritance is still worth a fair bit, I imagine. She wasn't at Keira Lambie's funeral, and there are suggestions that Beth and her brother didn't get on."

He nodded towards Dharwan. "Go round the neighbours again, but this time ask about visitors to the house; people who didn't seem suspicious at the time."

"Yes, sir," said Dharwan.

"However," McCord continued, "we must also consider the possibility that somebody swapped the meds while they were meeting Lambie somewhere else."

He moved to Pamela Boyd's picture that he had duplicated from the board to the right. "If Jordan Lambie and Pamela Boyd had an affair, and that's a big 'if' in my opinion, she would have had plenty opportunity."

"But what about motive?" Calderwood asked. "Did she start the affair with the intention of killing him in order to stop the project? That would be pretty extreme. Or could it have been jealousy?"

"Your guess is as good as mine," McCord said.

"Another person we have not considered in connection with the Lambies is Sean Listerman." McCord tapped on the butcher's ruddy face that smiled genially at them from the board. "Apparently, he was Jordan Lambie's oldest, and as far as we know, only friend, but things weren't all lovey-dovey between them either."

"Was he not part of this dodgy land deal?" Turner asked.

"He was," McCord said. "Listerman had agreed to sell his land to Lambie for the solar panel project, but then withdrew, leaving Lambie in the lurch. That being the case, one would expect Lambie to have killed him, rather than the other way round, but we need to check him out."

He raised his voice as the officers had started speculating about these possibilities. "And with all the excitement, don't forget Anthony Upshaw. He is still a suspect for Keira Lambie's murder and a man I'd like to see behind bars for a very long time, for what he did to her in Glasgow if nothing else. Chop chop. I want some results by the time Calderwood and I are back from our chat with Beth Lambie."

Chapter 21

Much to McCord's annoyance, they had to drive all the way to the Port of Leith, where the office of Lambie's Marine Services was located. This time, Gilchrist had decreed, McCord would not haul grieving relatives into his police station and subject them to spurious accusations of murder as he was wont to do.

The superintendent had also insisted on Calderwood going with McCord to counterbalance his lack of tact when dealing with respectable and well-heeled members of the public. This, on the other hand, suited McCord fine as he had become used to the tempering presence of his charming colleague, who always managed to calm the waters that McCord had happily stirred up.

They had chosen a good day for a trip to the harbour. The stiff breeze still carried some unseasonal warmth; the sea and the sky were in competition for which of them could produce the deepest, holiday-brochure blue, and even the massive barges in their bold colours were quite picturesque.

"I'd hate to be on one of those during a storm," Calderwood said. "Remember the RV Petrel?"

McCord pulled a face. "Of course."

The previous spring, not far from the spot where they were standing, the three-thousand-ton US Navy vessel had become dislodged from her holdings during a storm and tipped to a precarious angle. A major incident was declared, swallowing up the city's resources. It had taken several weeks to right and refloat the vessel, and McCord guessed that the resulting compensation claims were still filling the pockets of lawyers.

On the ubiquitous iron railings and steel structures whose functions eluded McCord, sat long rows of gulls as if they owned the place. With a mixture of awe and repulsion, he spotted among them a great black-backed gull; the king of the coast and a merciless pirate so large that it could swallow whole puffin chicks and other young birds.

As McCord and Calderwood walked towards their destination, they were passed by burly men in hi-vis vests and hard hats who were going purposefully about their business, talking to each other in a lingo that McCord did not understand.

Squatting only fifty yards from the quayside, the main office of Lambie's Marine Services was a modest, low-slung building whose architecture was determined by functionality rather than aesthetics. McCord suspected that it dated from the times of the company's founder, Lambie senior, who had started a small ship repair service in the eighties and subsequently added subsidiaries in Aberdeen and Greenock, making his company a major player in the field.

They had hardly opened the door when a flash of brown and white shot towards them. Before McCord could react, two paws dug into his thighs and a long, rough tongue was licking his chin.

"Down, Boyo, down!" an irritated voice shouted.

It had no effect whatsoever on the boxer, who was clearly delighted to see them.

Calderwood, seeing his boss's discomfort, patted his shins to coax the dog over to him and stroked the side of its head, skilfully keeping it away from his tailor-made suit.

"Good boy," he said, when it had calmed down. "Good boy."

"He's just a menace," the middle-aged, homely-looking woman in the office said apologetically. "Aren't you, you monster!" She gave the dog a cuddle and sent him sternly back under her desk. His head down, the dog reluctantly obeyed.

McCord waited until the creature had settled on the low-pile carpet before he pulled out his warrant card.

"DI McCord and DS Calderwood. We'd like to talk to Beth Lambie. We spoke on the phone earlier."

"Ah, yes, of course. I hope you're not going to charge us under the Dangerous Dogs Act," she said with a giggle.

McCord had been thinking exactly along those lines, but Calderwood laughed.

"Boxers are such big softies. How old is he?"

"He's going to be ten in November," the secretary said fondly, "but he still behaves like a puppy."

"Is Ms Lambie in?" McCord butted in, fed up with the doggy talk.

The secretary straightened her cardigan.

"I'm afraid Beth has been delayed. There's been a problem on one of the ships. Can I get you a coffee?"

Before McCord had a chance to point out the relative importance of a murder investigation compared to whatever problem a ship might have, Calderwood accepted the offer gracefully.

The secretary made an inviting gesture towards the two armchairs in front of the desk.

"Please have a seat. I'll be back in a tick."

She disappeared through an open door into a tiny kitchen.

Keeping a beady eye on Boyo, who peeked out from under the desk, quivering with eagerness to pounce again, McCord slowly sat down. He was not entirely comfortable with a large, exuberant dog in such close proximity to his crotch, but considering Boyo's indiscriminately affectionate nature, he suspected the worst that could happen was another lick.

After giving the beast a look that usually intimidated criminals and even tabloid journalists, he examined an atrocious oil painting depicting an older and male version of Beth Lambie. The same square jaw and a forehead like a mule.

"Don't you think it's strange that she's at work so soon after her brother has died?" McCord whispered.

"Some people find it easier to deal with grief when they keep themselves busy," Calderwood said mildly. "And if it was an emergency…"

He broke off as the secretary came back with a cafetière, three mugs, a milk jug and a plate of Fox's biscuits.

"What a tragedy about Jordan," she said, pouring the coffee into plain, white mugs. "His mother died of a heart attack as well. But at least she was forty-three, not twenty-six."

"Have you worked for the family long?" Calderwood asked.

"Twenty-two years," the secretary said proudly. "Not long after Mr Lambie had founded the firm. It was quite a small outfit then, and look at us now." She pointed at the painting. "He passed away earlier this year. What a shock that was! A stroke at the age of fifty-nine." She tutted. "I did tell him to go easy on the cooked breakfasts, but he always did what he wanted. Strong-minded he was, Mr Lambie; too stubborn for his own good if you ask me. Such a shame that they never got to make up."

She handed the little milk jug to McCord.

"Who, Mr Lambie senior and his wife?" Calderwood asked.

"Oh no, she was devoted to him, and he was devastated when she died, but he and Jordan never got on." She sadly shook her head. "Families, eh?"

McCord helped himself to a biscuit. This delay was turning out not too badly. It was always interesting to hear what long-term employees had to say about their employers, and the coffee was great.

"Is that why Ms Lambie is running the business now, and not her brother?" Calderwood continued his gentle probing.

"Yes, Jordan never wanted anything to do with his father or the business. He moved out straight after his mother died, while he was still at university. I suppose he should have stayed and supported his father and sister, but there was so much animosity between them…" She caught herself, looking embarrassed at speaking ill of the dead. "Mrs Lambie's death was a terrible blow for Jordan; they were very close, him and his mother."

"And he never tried to repair the relationship between himself and his father?" Calderwood asked.

She shook her head.

"Jordan stayed away for ages, and only came back after he got married to his first wife. Mr Lambie was quite taken with Melissa. 'At long last, Jordan got something right,' he said. She tried to reconcile them, but Jordan wouldn't hear of it, and then he and Melissa got divorced soon after."

Unable to hide her disapproval, she fell silent.

"So, Ms Lambie has been running the business since her father's death?" McCord asked.

The secretary brightened up. "Oh, Beth has been working here ever since she was sixteen. It's good to see somebody at the helm who loves the business as much as Mr Lambie did, but it's not been easy recently– ah, talk of the devil! How did you get on, Beth?"

Beth Lambie had breezed into the room. She was dressed in a black business suit and sensible shoes that were scuffed at the toes.

She had no time to reply as Boyo shot out from under the desk and jumped into her arms, almost toppling her over.

Beth Lambie seemed to share the dog's enthusiasm. "There's my buddy-boy, did you miss me?" she exclaimed, returning the slobbering kiss of the dog. "I missed you, too, my darling."

Not wanting to draw Boyo's attention to himself, McCord slowly put his biscuit down and stayed seated, but the dog was far too ecstatic to see his owner to care about anybody else in the room.

Eventually, both dog and owner had got over their joyous reunion, and Beth Lambie straightened up.

"Sorry I'm late. The dozy devils hadn't put on the new hatch cover properly."

Seeing McCord's blank face, she added, "It means that sea water can penetrate the hold of the ship and make it list or even sink. Not the kind of advertising I'm after."

She stretched out a hand to McCord who rose from his chair and shook it firmly.

"I'm Beth Lambie. You must be DI McCord and...?" She turned to Calderwood.

"DS Calderwood, pleased to meet you. We're very sorry about your brother but we have to ask you a few questions."

Her face betrayed no emotion. "Let's go into my office."

She opened the door to the left and deftly avoided falling over Boyo, who had anticipated her move and squeezed through the gap before them.

The office was generously proportioned but devoid of any homely touches apart from a framed photograph of Lambie senior on the solid oak desk. McCord registered the absence of any pictures of her mother or brother.

Boyo was circling the large, L-shaped desk, sniffing and whining in turn.

"He's still missing his daddy," Beth Lambie said.

"You used to have two dogs?" McCord asked, appalled at the mayhem that must have caused.

Beth Lambie gave him a funny look. "Boyo was my dad's dog," she said. "They were inseparable."

McCord took a moment to process this. "Ah."

"Please, take a seat."

Beth Lambie pointed to the two chairs in front of the desk, which looked only marginally more comfortable than the ones in the reception area. It was obvious that people did not hang around here to talk.

Beth Lambie lowered herself into the swivel chair behind the desk. Boyo collapsed at her feet with a sigh.

"Is the post-mortem done at last?" Beth Lambie clearly wasn't into polite preambles. "Surely, that wasn't necessary. It was well known that my bother suffered from severe congenital arrhythmia."

Calderwood exchanged a quick glance with McCord, establishing that he should start with his good-cop routine, which suited his natural kindness so well.

"Unfortunately, when somebody dies so suddenly, especially at your brother's age, it is routine to do a post-mortem," Calderwood explained.

Beth Lambie scowled. "I was wondering when I can start to make the funeral arrangements. It is quite upsetting to have this hanging over me."

"It must be," Calderwood said.

McCord shifted in his seat. It was time to ask some uncomfortable questions.

"Are you aware of your brother's will?"

Beth Lambie regarded him quizzically. "We hadn't discussed the matter," she said, "and the reading of the will hasn't happened yet, obviously."

"He left everything to his wife, Keira, but because she died before him and they had no children, his estate reverts to you as his nearest relative."

Beth Lambie frowned. "You opened his will? I don't understand why the police are involved in all this."

"We are involved because somebody swapped your brother's medicines for painkillers," McCord said, watching her closely. "We don't believe he did this himself, so we're treating his death as murder."

Beth Lambie stared at McCord and, after not being offered any other explanation, turned to Calderwood.

"Murder?"

"Yes, Ms Lambie," Calderwood confirmed. "I'm sorry."

McCord, on the other hand, was not sorry at all. "When did you last see your brother? I noticed you were not at Mrs Lambie's funeral."

Beth Lambie's expression hardened.

"I went to see him" – she checked the diary on her desk – "on the fourth," she said. "To give him my condolences."

"It took you two days to get round to that. Interesting. And why did you not go to your sister-in-law's funeral?" McCord asked. "More problems with hatch covers?"

Beth Lambie bristled. "You have no right to speak to me like that!"

"I have every right," McCord said. "I'm investigating a murder. Either you tell us now what's been going on between you and your brother, or we do this under caution at the station later."

Beth Lambie's blustering confidence had given way to a sudden eagerness to cooperate.

"There's no need for that. Of course, I'll cooperate fully with your investigation. I'm just totally shocked. Jordan murdered – and you are suspecting *me*?"

"I'm listening," McCord said, unmoved.

"After that terrible business with Keira, I thought he needed some time to process it all. Then I went over to offer him a job in the company. After his solar panel project had gone belly-up, I thought he could do with some support."

"That is very generous of you," McCord said. "What did your brother say?"

"He told me to eff off," Beth Lambie said. "And he made it clear he didn't want me to come to Keira's funeral, so I respected his wishes and stayed away."

"That's a pretty strong reaction to a friendly job offer," McCord said. "Can you explain that?"

Beth Lambie sighed. "Jordan and I never got on. I think he resented the fact that I was very close to our dad."

"And he wasn't?"

Beth Lambie shrugged. "Jordan was always a real mummy's boy, and when our mother died, he completely went to pieces and blamed Dad for her death. It was ridiculous, of course," she added hastily. "There's nothing Dad could have done. He worked a lot; well, you have to if you're running a business. Jordan never understood that. He was attending a few lectures at uni and thought he was a martyr. Dad was devastated when our mother died, but he didn't wear his heart on his sleeve like Jordan did. They simply didn't seem to be able to communicate."

"And you were quite happy to take on the business," McCord stated.

Beth Lambie shrugged again.

"I've never wanted to do anything else. I left school when I was sixteen, just like Dad, and started working for the company. Dad showed me the ropes and gave me more and more responsibility over the years."

She pointed at Lambie senior's photograph, and McCord saw her eyes fill with tears. "He was a great man," she said quietly, "and he suffered because Jordan was such a disappointment to him. Dad was always so strong, and Jordan... wasn't."

"It depends how you define 'strong'," McCord said. "Would it surprise you to learn that at his wife's funeral he killed a friend of hers?"

Beth Lambie's eyes swivelled from the photograph to McCord.

"What? You think *Jordan* killed that woman?"

"We have plenty of evidence," McCord said. "That makes us think, of course, that he might have killed his wife as well. Do you think that is possible?"

McCord predicted she would shrug, and he was right. It seemed to be her only reaction to anything to do with her brother.

"If you'd asked me before, I'd have said no. Jordan adored Keira. God knows why. Don't get me wrong, she was a nice girl, but it was as if he'd signed his whole life over to her."

"Isn't that what marriage is supposed to be about?" Calderwood asked.

Beth Lambie gave yet another shrug. "Jordan stuck to Keira even though Dad tried to convince him that he was making a big mistake taking up with her."

"And was he?" McCord asked. "Making a mistake, I mean?"

"I had the impression they were very happy together. I was glad for Jordan that he had finally found the right person after it all went so horribly wrong with Melissa. His first wife," she added.

"Why did that marriage not work out?" McCord asked. "I heard that your dad was quite enamoured with her."

"Pah," she said bitterly. "He was fooled by Melissa's interest in the business. The problem for Jordan was that it was all she was interested in. When she met Jordan and found out about his background, she probably saw herself as the future First Lady of Lambie's Marine Services. She was badgering Jordan to go back into the business, and she was sucking up to Dad big time. It was cringeworthy, and Dad actually fell for it. Even clever men can be so stupid sometimes."

Calderwood's mouth twitched as he glanced at his boss, but McCord did not notice as he was too busy imagining Melissa Lambie coming up against her steely sister-in-law.

"And how did your brother feel about Melissa's plans?" he asked.

Beth Lambie smiled for the first time. "Jordan wasn't having it. He was working for one of the big energy companies at the time, but he really wanted to start his own business. We all thought it was pie in the sky, and he did make a mess of it in the end, didn't he? I think, when Melissa realised that Jordan would never be a success, she went off to find a more promising partner elsewhere."

"And how did Jordan react to that?" McCord asked.

Beth Lambie made no effort to disguise her contempt, both for the stupid question and for her brother's reaction.

"What do you think? He was incredibly bitter. He must have felt betrayed. But then, I always thought he used her as well; it was his way of getting away from home and creating a life for himself. They were far too young to get married, of course."

"You're not married yourself, Ms Lambie?" McCord asked although he knew the answer.

"No time for romance," Beth Lambie said with a little laugh. "Running a business is never a nine-to-five job, and with the way the economy is at the moment, it is a battle to keep afloat. If you'll excuse me now, I need to deal with some suppliers."

McCord and Calderwood rose.

"Thank you for giving us so much of your precious time, Ms Lambie," McCord said, but his irony was lost on her. "If you can think of anything else you might have forgotten to mention, here is my card."

Chapter 22

Amy was on her second latte when Aiden Springfield arrived at the Marks & Spencer Café in Princes Street he had suggested as their meeting point. He nervously looked over his shoulder as he entered and scanned the room until he saw Amy wave at him from a table in the corner.

"I'm sorry, I'm late," he said, collapsing on the chair, "but there was a guy in a hoodie on the bus. I couldn't see his face, so I got off and took the next bus. I'm not sure it was Upshaw, but–"

"Don't worry, you're safe here," Amy said soothingly, taking in his unkempt ponytail and sallow complexion. If Springfield was afraid of every man in a hoodie in Edinburgh, it wouldn't be long until he ended up in psychiatric care. "What can I get you?"

Springfield jumped up. "I didn't mean for you to get my drink, I'll–"

"Relax," Amy said with a smile. "My treat. Peppermint tea and a vegan cake?" she guessed.

Springfield nodded gratefully and sank back into his chair.

While she was queuing, she pretended to study the menu, but threw furtive glances in Springfield's direction.

He was keeping an eye on the entrance and scrutinised every new customer.

"That's amazing, thank you," Springfield said when Amy returned with a tray. "I haven't been out much recently."

"Not even to The Green Fist?" Amy asked.

Springfield shook his head. "There's no point. With Keira and Pamela gone, the heart has been ripped out of the group. And Donnie… well, you know, we don't get on so well."

"Yes, I had that impression," Amy said, thinking back to her meeting with them at The Green Fist. Accusing people of murder was not the best way to make friends.

There was no room to get rid of the tray, so Amy pushed Springfield's cup and coconut slice towards him and started buttering her scone.

"Has Upshaw actually been in touch with you?" she asked. "Or have you seen him?"

Springfield bounced his teabag up and down in the hot water, watching it turn green. "No, but he is very clever. Keira never saw him either and still…"

He cleared his throat, close to tears. Then a thought occurred to him. "Has he been following you?" he asked.

"No, why would he? I've got nothing–"

She stopped herself. She needed to be more careful.

"–to do with this?" Springfield finished her sentence. "You're a member of The Green Fist; you're a young and attractive woman. Now that Keira is dead, he might get fixated on you. When you called, I was hoping…"

"That he was stalking me?" Amy said, attempting a humorous tone. "Thank you very much."

Springfield held up his hands, mortified. "No, of course not, but I thought if it was the two of us, the police would do something. This detective inspector basically told me to fight this monster on my own. I can't go on like this much longer!"

"If he thought you were in serious danger, he would arrange protection," Amy said with conviction, hastily adding, "I'm sure."

Springfield fell silent and moodily contemplated his brew. Amy suspected that he saw Upshaw behind every lamp post, while the man himself sat in his flat, his every move monitored by his mother.

There was nothing else to be gained from Springfield, but Amy felt sorry for him, and to distract him from his paranoia, she asked him about his poetry. She soon regretted her kindness, however, as she was given an emotional recital of his latest work, a two-page, soulful reminiscence of Keira's affinity with nature ending with her physical manifestation rejoining the earth while her spirit remained alive in the flowers, the trees, the river and the wind.

"Do you know what's going to happen to Keira's ashes now that her husband is dead?" he asked Amy, draining his cup and finishing off the cake. "There is nobody left in the world who cared about her apart from me."

"And Declan Carr," Amy said.

Springfield waved the suggestion away. "He let Keira down like everybody else. He's just on a guilt trip and he'll forget all about it as soon as he needs the next hit."

The remark struck Amy as uncharacteristically harsh, but then, Springfield was grieving. "Why don't you get in touch with the crematorium and ask?"

She had the feeling that the officer there would like nothing better than to be relieved of the last reminder of the worst day of his life.

Pleased to see that, despite his broken heart, Springfield's appetite had not suffered, Amy stacked their plates and made to leave. Springfield rose and put the notebook with his poems in his jacket pocket.

"Are you going back to Heriot-Watt?" he asked as they descended the stairs. "We could go some of the way together."

"No, I'm staying in town tonight," Amy said, who feared a rendition of more poems on the long bus journey out west.

Springfield regarded her intensely with his liquid eyes.

"I thought you wrote on your application form that you stayed on campus."

"Yes," Amy said a little too quickly, "but I'm meeting my aunt later. She's having a difficult time."

He looked disappointed. "I'm sorry to hear that. Thanks for the invitation."

"You're very welcome. It was good to see you, Aiden."

"And you. Be careful on your way home."

She watched him walk towards the bus stop, but when he turned round, she pretended to read something on her phone.

Chapter 23

Sean Listerman had readily agreed to come in to St Leonard's police station after business hours but, having crawled through the city centre during the rush hour, his nerves were in shreds even before he was told that his old school friend had been murdered. The news made him break out in a sweat that stained his armpits and made his round face glisten in the harsh strip light of Interview Room 2.

"I can't believe it," he said for the third time when Calderwood handed him a glass of water.

"Mr Listerman, I'm not making this up," McCord said with more than a hint of impatience. "Can you tell us when you last saw Mr Lambie alive?"

Listerman took a gulp of the water. "At Keira's funeral, of course," he said. "I gave a statement to one of your officers then."

"I meant before that day, obviously," McCord said.

"Ehm, I went to see him the day after poor Keira died, no, two days after, I can't remember, it's all such a blur," Listerman babbled, wiping damp hands on the corduroy trousers that stuck to his bulging thighs.

"Where was this?"

"At the Riccarton Inn," Listerman said, more assuredly now.

"And?" McCord prompted. "What did you talk about?"

"I wanted to make up with him because we'd fallen out. And I wanted to tell him how sorry I was about Keira. He loved her so much. Tragic it is, simply tragic."

Seeing McCord's face, he quickly moved on. "We were best pals, you know, at school. The odd couple, the teachers called us. Some of the other children were not very nice. They bullied me because of my weight and Jordan because of his stammer."

McCord was about to interrupt when he noticed Calderwood leaning forward, silently encouraging Listerman to go on.

"Once they were particularly mean to me, and Jordan suddenly went for them although they were three against us – well, I was no use, I was an absolute coward, still am, to be honest, so it was him against three, but he was in such a fury, he started punching and kicking them, and I'm sure he bit one of them in the arm. And that bastard, excuse my language, had the cheek to complain later that he'd been assaulted. But our form teacher knew what these other boys were like and told them to shut up, and from then on, they left us in peace. That day, Jordan saved me from endless misery."

"No wonder you were very fond of him," Calderwood said.

Listerman nodded vigorously. "That's why I agreed immediately when he asked me to sell him the land I had inherited from my grandfather. This solar energy project seemed very important to him, so I said yes before I'd asked my wife, and that was a big mistake."

"Did she persuade you to withdraw from the arrangement?"

"I didn't need persuading," Listerman said. "When word got out, Pamela Boyd turned up – oh my God, she is dead now as well… What is going on? It used to be such a nice little community–"

McCord brusquely brought him back to the point. "What did Pamela Boyd say to you?"

"She came to the shop and told me all those horrible things about solar panels… I had no idea, I always thought they were brilliant, and I had promised Jordan to sell my land, but then she said that she would make sure that people didn't buy their meat from me anymore because it was my fault that the area was about to be destroyed, and she would tell everybody that I put offal into my sausages. I don't know how she found out about that, I didn't tell a soul because it puts people off, but it's actually quite healthy, and you have no idea what overheads–"

McCord slapped the desk to stop Listerman's stream of verbal diarrhoea.

"So, you broke your promise to your best friend and told him he couldn't have your land. When was this?"

Listerman hung his head.

"At the beginning of August. I am ashamed of that but what was I supposed to do? I have a family to support!"

"And how did Mr Lambie react?" McCord asked.

"Very badly. I mean, I expected him to be angry, but I thought he would understand why I had to do it. He didn't. He even told me he'd take me to court over it. To court! It had only been an informal agreement; we hadn't signed a contract or anything, but he said in Scotland a verbal agreement is binding and he wouldn't let me wriggle out of it."

"That sounds like a strong motive for murder," McCord said. "A lawsuit, especially one you might lose, wouldn't have helped your standing in the community or your finances. So, you swap his meds and wait for your problem to go away…"

"Now hang on a minute," Listerman shrieked. "What do you mean about swapping his meds? You're not suggesting that I killed Jordan? My best pal?"

"You destroyed your best pal's dream," McCord said, "because without your land, the project wasn't viable anymore."

"But, but," Listerman spluttered, "I thought he could buy some other land for his project, and he did, from Donnie Murray. It's not my fault that they didn't stick to the rules and got caught."

McCord was not ready to let Listerman off the hook yet.

"So, after your best pal's wife had died and his project had gone down the pan, mainly because of you, you went to see him to make sure he would drop the lawsuit. But when he wouldn't forgive you, you simply left him to die."

"No!" Listerman wailed. "I'd never kill Jordan! He looked awful that day at the Riccarton Inn, but I thought it was because he was grieving. I swear I had nothing to do with his death!"

Listerman anxiously watched as McCord sat for a moment, pondering what he had heard and then slowly rose from his chair. "You're free to go… for now. We will check what you've told us, and then we'll probably need to speak to you again, so don't leave Edinburgh without letting us know. DS Calderwood will see you out."

Listerman stood up, his knees barely supporting him. "I swear—"

"Goodbye, Mr Listerman," McCord said and made some notes on the file.

When Calderwood reappeared at the office a few minutes later, McCord was sitting at this desk, his chin resting on his folded hands.

"What do you think, Calderwood?"

"He had motive and opportunity. But if he swapped the pills when they first fell out, Listerman would have had to take the painkillers with him. He didn't even know that Lambie was thinking of suing him at the time, though. Nobody plans a murder just in case."

"Unless they spoke before Listerman's visit," McCord said, "and he came ready with the painkillers."

"But would Lambie have lasted as long as that without his meds?" Calderwood asked. "They fell out at the beginning of August. That's almost six weeks before Lambie died."

"Good point," McCord said. "Check the timings with Lambie's GP. What if Listerman swapped the meds during his second visit, at the Riccarton Inn?"

Calderwood nodded. "Perhaps. I had another thought, though."

"Yes?" McCord asked, keen to hear anything that might help him out of this muddle of murders.

"What if he is lying about the timings and he turned up on the evening Keira died and not afterwards? What if he was the one who frightened her and caused her to fall?"

"Would she be frightened of him?" McCord asked doubtfully. "He admits to being a complete coward, and I think this is an accurate description. Secretly changing meds, yes, but breaking in and threatening or attacking a woman?"

"But what if Keira caught him swapping the meds in the bathroom or the bedroom? Then he would have had to shut her up."

"It is possible," McCord conceded. "We need to check his alibi. Tell your fiancée to take a picture of Listerman and his car when she goes round the Lambies' neighbours. With him being a friend in the past, he would not have registered with them as being potentially dangerous."

McCord's phone pinged and his face lit up.

"Sutton has something for me."

He ran across to her workstation, knocked and waited until he was admitted.

"What have you got?" he asked, trying to hide his desperation.

"No communications between Jordan Lambie and Pamela Boyd."

"None?" McCord asked, perplexed. "Nothing at all?"

Sutton regarded him with confusion in her huge eyes. Normally, she didn't have to repeat things unnecessarily. "Nothing," she humoured him. "And no messages to his phone during the funeral."

Disappointed, McCord was about to thank her when she added, "But this."

She handed him a few printed sheets and turned back to her computer.

McCord scanned the first page and smiled grimly.

"You are brilliant."

Only a twitch round the corners of her mouth told him that she had heard and appreciated the praise.

McCord rushed out of her labyrinthine den and waved the printouts at Calderwood, who was waiting outside.

"Emails between Jordan and the family lawyer after their father's will had been read. Lambie senior wanted the whole company and the family home to go to Beth; Jordan was to get only the private cash and some of the other investments, in total fifty thousand pounds. He argued that Jordan had never contributed to the business, so he could not expect to profit from it, and he expected his son to at least respect his dying wish after being such a disappointment to him. However, Jordan planned to contest the will. He wanted half of all the assets."

"Would he have had success with that?" Calderwood asked.

McCord nodded. "In Scotland, parents can't disinherit their children, so he would have won his case. With Jordan now dead, his sister owns the whole company and all other assets. People have killed for much less. Get onto the lab and see if they found any fingerprints on the bottle of pills. And then bring Beth Lambie back in."

* * *

"Mmm… mmm! Mmmm!"

Valerie was temporarily muted by a couple of pins in her mouth. She had wrapped printed cotton fabric for Amy's new dress around her waist and marked the spot with a pencil, so Amy grasped the opportunity to get her point across.

"I'm telling you, Mum, it isn't a date. Not really," she said.

Martin had persuaded Valerie that it wouldn't do her reputation any good if her daughter attended a wedding in a T-shirt and a pleated rug, but this had necessitated telling her about the plus-one arrangement in the first place, which had triggered her deep-seated anxieties about Amy's involvement with crime in general and DI McCord in particular.

"McCord only wants to please his dad, so I thought I'd do him a favour," Amy said. "And anyway," she added testily, "there would be nothing wrong with a date."

Martin's attempts at matchmaking had always provoked Amy into a cynical denial of even the remotest possibility of a romance between her and McCord, but to her surprise, she found that her mother's disapproval achieved the opposite. Why were they always meddling in her private affairs? It was her business, and nobody else's, who she went out with; even though she had to admit that, so far, her independent attempts had not been met with great success.

"Hmmm!" Valerie was clearly not convinced.

Choking on the feelings that she was unable to vent, she plucked the needles out of her mouth and stuck them onto a pin cushion as if it was a voodoo doll with McCord's face on it.

"What's the matter with that man?" she asked, finally able to speak. "Ever since he's been around, you've ended up in dangerous situations. Dead bodies, murderers on the loose; even a birdwatching trip turns into a ferry disaster when he's there."

"That's not fair, Mum," Amy said heatedly. "You can hardly blame him for the cancellation of a ferry because of a storm. And stop blowing things out of all proportion; it wasn't a disaster at all." It had been, in a way, but Martin had laid the blame firmly at her door.

Valerie, who was kneeling on the floor, muttered something unintelligible, while checking the measurements in several places as Amy slowly turned in a circle.

"McCord did his level best to keep me away from the crimes he was investigating," Amy said, "but I *wanted* to be part of his investigations. And he saved me more than once, remember?"

"I do remember," Valerie said, shuddering.

"Anyway, I'm going to a wedding with him, not a crime scene."

"That's another point. Who asks a gorgeous girl out as a favour to his dad? It's an insult. He should be on his knees begging you to come."

Amy grinned at the absurd notion. "That's just not McCord. If he did, I wouldn't know what to say."

"'Bugger off' would do nicely," Valerie said.

She made a move to get up, but her knees had gone stiff and creaked alarmingly.

Amy grabbed her arm and, laughing, gave an exaggerated heave.

"Cheer up, Mum. I really appreciate you making me a new dress when you're so busy. You always make me look amazing, and everything is going to be fine."

Valerie muttered something Amy did not catch, and perhaps it was better that way.

Chapter 24

Away from her home turf and seated at a Formica table in a bare interview room, Beth Lambie held herself stiffly upright on the uncomfortable plastic chair with her arms defiantly folded over her chest. Forensics had found no useable fingerprints on Jordan Lambie's pill bottle, so McCord had no choice but to crack on with what he had.

He placed the sheets Sutton had given him carefully in front of her, so that she could see that there was no point in denying facts.

"We've found some email correspondence between you and your brother. Why didn't you tell us he was going to force you to sell the company?"

Beth Lambie raised her chin. "You didn't ask."

Calderwood shook his head.

"It would have been much better for you if you had been open with us. It looks suspicious if you withhold important information."

"I didn't know that this was important," Beth Lambie retorted. "I had nothing to do with my brother's death."

McCord lifted the email lying on top of the pile and pretended to read it.

"You were pretty much begging him to leave the company intact," he said eventually. "You offered him shares in lieu, but he insisted on a full payout."

Beth Lambie nodded. "That is correct."

"You must have been very angry," Calderwood said with sympathy.

"Do you think?" she flared up, righteous indignation making her throw caution to the wind. "Jordan broke Dad's heart; always siding with our mother, and after her death, treating Dad as if it was his fault."

"I wonder if it was," McCord asked, deliberately provoking her. "If your mother was very ill, perhaps she needed more care than your father was willing to give her?"

Beth Lambie slapped her hands on the table and leaned forward. "My mother had been unwell for a while, but things were tough during Covid, and Dad was doing his best to keep us afloat."

Unaware of the pun, she rattled on.

"Jordan never stirred a finger for the business, and then he has the cheek to ignore Dad's wishes and try to force me to destroy the company Dad had built from scratch. Yes, that was my dear brother to a T. Me, me, me, all the way."

McCord quickly pushed on. If Beth Lambie was in a mood for confidences, he was not going to stop her.

"So, when you went to visit him, your generous offer of a job and shares was nothing more than a roundabout way to give him what was legally his anyway?"

"'The law is an ass,' I believe is the phrase," Beth Lambie said bitterly. "But yes, when Jordan's project crashed and burned, I saw a chance to find a mutually agreeable arrangement. I guess, I hoped that he would finally see how precious a family business is."

Her voice became hoarse, and she struggled to regain her composure.

"The idea was that I would keep the house and control of the company, but he would get his share even if it wasn't in ready cash. Given time, I would have been able to buy him out. I even offered him a job, which *was* generous after *Forth Write* magazine exposed him as a cheat."

"And your brother didn't accept the offer?" Calderwood asked in a tone suggesting that any reasonable person would have done so.

"No, he insisted on the payout although it wasn't in his financial interest in the long term. I'm sure he did it just to spite me and Dad. He'd have turned in his grave. I don't know why I expected anything different from Jordan."

"But now, with him out of the way," McCord said, "the company, house and all your father's assets are yours alone."

Beth Lambie stabbed a finger at McCord. "I know what you are implying, but you're wrong." She turned to Calderwood. "You wanted me to be honest, and I'm not going to pretend to be devastated by grief. Jordan and I didn't get on, but I didn't kill him." She jutted out her chin. "Can I go now?"

McCord would have liked nothing better than to throw Beth Lambie into a cell, but without any evidence to charge her, he had no choice but to let her go.

"For now, Ms Lambie," he said. "But let us know if you leave town."

* * *

It was a dull evening, and McCord got up to turn on the lights when Calderwood put on his jacket. McCord looked up at the office clock.

"You're away sharp," he said, "but I suppose you're desperate to get home to your fiancée. Any plans?"

"Today is exactly six months since our first date." Calderwood's face glowed. "The perfect excuse for a romantic evening in. But I need to get some more scented candles on the way home. Surina likes the place to be a real fire hazard."

"Candles," McCord repeated as if this concept was new to him. He began to pace up and down while he was thinking. "Of course, why weren't the candles lit if they were having a romantic evening?"

"Sorry? Whose candles are we talking about now?" Calderwood asked, puzzled.

"The Lambies," McCord said. "Jordan Lambie told me the fire was lit because they were, you know, but then they would have lit the candles as well, wouldn't they?"

Calderwood nodded. "If Keira Lambie was anything like Surina, definitely."

McCord stood still.

"So, what if the fire hadn't been lit for romantic purposes at all but to burn something?"

"Like what?" Calderwood asked.

But McCord had already moved on. "Is the Lambies' place still closed off?"

"No, forensics have finished, but the house can't be sold until the investigation–"

McCord was not listening anymore. He grabbed the receiver of the office phone and dialled the number of Wester Hailes police station.

"DI McCord here, from St Leonard's … I need somebody to go 5 Caulderhame Road in Currie … Yes, the Lambie case … If the ashes from that evening are still in the wood burner, have them bagged up and sent to forensics to check if something other than wood was burned there … Yes, now. Thanks."

He put the phone down and noticed Calderwood, who was hovering by the door. "What are you still doing here? Off you go!"

Chapter 25

"Stop staring at me," Amy snapped at Martin.

He had driven her to Upshaw's place of work, the world-famous Tunnock's factory in Uddingston, a large, drab building brightened up by bold red lettering and their iconic logo proudly announcing that Thomas Tunnock had started the thriving business in 1890.

They had positioned themselves opposite the back entrance where the employees would leave the building at the end of their shift.

After Amy had told Martin about her conversation with Aiden Springfield, he had guessed correctly that Amy intended to speak to Upshaw face to face. Using all his diplomatic finesse and eventually even blackmail, Martin had persuaded Amy that he should accompany her for her safety, and although his bright-yellow Mini was not exactly blending in at the car park, it was a lot less conspicuous than the MG would have been.

"I would still recognise you," Martin said.

His fretting made Amy nervous. "It's my nose, isn't it?"

Amy's long, aquiline nose was nature's way of signalling her innate curiosity, and all she could do to distract attention from it was by wearing thick-rimmed, coloured glasses.

"Your nose is beautiful," Martin declared with conviction, and Amy couldn't help but smile at her biggest fan.

In order to make sure that Upshaw would not get an inkling who she was, she had spent all day transforming herself into a curvy blonde, praying that the hair dye would come out in time for Keith and Clare's wedding. Her first attempt at padding using bubble wrap had failed because of the noise it made any time she moved; in the end, she had filled an E cup bra with cotton wool and wrapped about a hundred yards of bandaging round herself.

Amy would have liked to wear one of her mother's outfits, but since Valerie lived with John now, it was too dangerous to nick one out of her wardrobe and put it back unnoticed. Amy was far more scared of her mother's reaction to finding out Amy was meeting a stalker and potential killer than of the stalker and potential killer himself. So, she had gone to a charity shop and bought a loose denim dress that hid the tell-tale horizontal lines running across her body.

"How do you know he's been working this shift?" Martin asked.

"I phoned the office claiming to be his mother and asked when he would be finished today," Amy said. "They were most obliging. Mrs Upshaw probably threatened to sue them if they treated him as anything but a persecuted innocent."

"If Upshaw hasn't bothered any of the employees, they don't have sufficient grounds for his dismissal," Martin said, "at least until he has been formally charged."

The hands of the clock neared five. He put a tweed cap over his suspiciously black hair and buttoned up the beige raincoat to cover the bright, floral kaftan he was wearing.

"I feel utterly ridiculous in this outfit," he said.

Amy grinned. "You look like most men in their fifties."

"Exactly!"

"There he is!" Amy pointed to the entrance where a group of workers had spilled out; behind them, slowly, on his own, walked Anthony Upshaw. She swung open the car door.

"Wish me luck!"

"Be careful!" Martin twittered in alarm. "Don't go anywhere with him unless it's the Tinto Tapas, as planned!"

"Yes, yes," Amy said, already halfway across the lane. "Mr Upshaw?"

Upshaw frowned suspiciously. "Who wants to know?"

"I'm Simone. I used to work with Keira at the café. I–"

"I don't want to talk about her. Go away," he said, accelerating his pace, eyes darting around him as if he was afraid of an attack.

"I don't believe you're guilty of anything," Amy said quickly. "I think you are a victim as much as she was. Isn't that right?"

Upshaw stopped in his tracks to face her. For a moment, Amy was afraid he would laugh at her disguise, but he didn't look at her properly at all; he kept checking the car park behind her.

"You're damn right. All I did was love her. How's that a crime?"

"Love is never a crime," Amy said emphatically. "I can see how much you're grieving for her. So, what went wrong?"

"Everybody was against us," he said, and she could sense the anger boiling just under the surface.

Suddenly, Amy was glad to know Martin was just twenty yards away and, no doubt, watching their every move.

"Who do you mean?" Amy asked.

"Everybody!" Upshaw shouted now. "Her so-called friends who told her to go to the police. They accused me of all sorts when I was only trying to make her see that we belonged together. Then my mother…" He stopped, afraid to say more.

"Your mother?" Amy prompted gently.

After another 360-degree scan of the car park, he continued.

"She never liked Keira. From the word go she tried to drive us apart. She even bribed her to stay away from me!"

"Your mother drove you apart? That's terrible!" Amy clapped her hand over her mouth in a pretence of shock.

"Yes! Keira belonged to me!"

All the dams had broken. With tears in his eyes, Upshaw stamped his foot on the broken tarmac. "And because of her, Keira ran away and hid – from *me*!" He gave a bitter laugh. "She must have been so frightened and confused, she even got married! And then there was this long-haired hippie who was coming on to her as well, when all the time she should have been with *me*!"

"That must have been so hard for you," Amy said, doing her level best to look sympathetic. "And what happened the night she died? Were you there?"

Upshaw winced. "I–"

"Excuse me, who are you?" a chilly voice sounded next to them.

Upshaw spun round and stumbled backwards.

Amy eyed the woman who had pulled herself up to her full height and was looking down at Amy like a bird of prey ready to attack a mouse.

Amy recognised the sharp features and immaculately coiffed head from the crematorium car park.

"I'm a colleague," she improvised. "And you must be Anthony's mother. Pleased to meet you."

She stretched out a hand that was ignored.

"It's time we were away," Patricia Upshaw told her son, and walked briskly towards her Audi.

Upshaw followed reluctantly and shot Amy a furtive glance before lowering himself into the passenger seat and slamming the door shut as the car pulled away.

Once they were out of sight, Amy ran back to Martin's Mini and wriggled herself into the passenger seat.

"And?" Martin twittered excitedly. "Please tell me he didn't recognise you?"

She shook her head. "He's completely wrapped up in his own world. Complete nutter. I'm sure he stalked Keira, and he was about to tell me about killing her when the bloody mother arrived. He's terrified of her, and no wonder. I bet she knows exactly what he was up to and she's doing everything she can to keep him out of prison, just like the last time."

Martin shuddered. "He looked furious. I was about to come over to get you away from him. You must tell DI McCord."

Amy nodded. "I'll call him right now. Ironically, I think that everybody is safe for now. His mother will make sure he's not going to put a foot wrong until the investigation is over."

Chapter 26

"I wondered if you'd come in today," Calderwood said to McCord when he arrived at St Leonard's in the morning. "Most people would have taken the whole day off if they were going to a family wedding."

"I'm desperate to get this case wrapped up before I go," McCord said, "or at least make some progress. Where are we with Sean Listerman's alibi?"

"His wife confirmed that he was at home on the evening Keira Lambie died. She said he went to see Jordan Lambie at the Riccarton Inn two days later and came back very depressed. According to her, he felt very bad about letting his old friend down, and Keira's death had been a great shock. He had hoped to make up with Lambie and support him in his hour of need, but Lambie hadn't even let him into the room."

"Did you find her credible?" McCord asked.

Calderwood nodded. "The landlord at the Riccarton Inn remembers Listerman turning up on that day and leaving very shortly afterwards."

"So, if he swapped the pills, he must have done it at the beginning of August when they first fell out," McCord said.

Calderwood shook his head.

"I've checked with the Lambies' GP; he thinks it is very unlikely that Jordan Lambie would have lasted that long without his medication. Anyway, Listerman's motive has gone."

"Why?" McCord asked.

"There is no record of any lawsuit filed against Listerman by Jordan Lambie. He must have given up on the idea once Donald Murray sold him his land."

"Another dead end," McCord said despondently. "And I'm not sure what to make of this either." He pointed to his screen. "The forensic report on the ashes has come back. Apart from the type of wood that was sitting in the basket next to the burner, a lot of paper was burned; more than one would use to get the fire going. Most of the paper had been glossy, the type used for magazines."

Calderwood's eyes widened. "You're thinking…"

"I'm thinking that environmentally conscious people like the Lambies don't buy glossy magazines in the first place, and if they do, they recycle rather than burn them. Which means that either Keira or Jordan Lambie didn't want this magazine to be found…" McCord suddenly brightened up. "Hang on."

He picked up his phone, dialled Amy's number and put her on loudspeaker.

"Amy? Could you check if the Lambies subscribed to *Forth Write*?"

"I've taken the day off for the wedding, haven't you? Obviously not," she answered her own question. "Hold on, I can get into our files from my laptop as well."

There was a pause while Amy called up the list.

"No, neither of them was a subscriber. Why?"

"One of the Lambies, or both, burnt a magazine on the evening of her death. Shame. I thought…"

"You wondered if it was ours?"

"Yes," he said. "Damn."

There was a pause. McCord could almost hear Amy's brain cells going into overdrive.

"But it must have been!" Amy exclaimed. "That day, with Martin's article, Jordan Lambie's whole project went bust. It can't be a coincidence." McCord heard her pacing up and down.

"Maybe Keira Lambie saw the story on the cover and burned the magazine to save their romantic evening," Calderwood suggested.

"No, no," Amy said. "The story was splashed all over the cover. If she'd bought the magazine at a newsagent's, she would have noticed the cover story straightaway; same for Jordan Lambie–"

Calderwood sighed. "True."

"But," Amy said slowly, "if neither of them bought it, someone else must have dropped it off that evening. Someone who wanted to warn them about the scandal that would be all over the news the following morning."

"There weren't many people who wished Jordan Lambie well," McCord pointed out. "Sean Listerman? But he was at home that evening, according to his wife. Donald Murray? He would be directly affected by the scandal, and he would have wanted to get his story straight with Jordan Lambie before the police came knocking on his door. Perhaps he went to their house, found them gone and left the magazine to warn him."

"That makes sense," Amy said. "Why don't you check with Murray and see what he says?"

"I'd never have thought of that," McCord said with a deadpan expression. "And yes, of course, I'll keep you posted."

He put his phone down and saw Calderwood's grin.

"What?"

"You're such a good team," Calderwood said.

"Ach, shut up," McCord snapped, but it did not sound convincing.

He checked on his computer and dialled a number.

"Mr Murray? DI McCord here. Could you clear up something for us?"

"Happy to help, DI McCord." Murray sounded eager to get into McCord's good books. "What would you like to know?"

"Did you leave a copy of *Forth Write* magazine at the Lambies' house on the evening Mrs Lambie died?"

There was a pause. "What a strange question, but I'm sure you have your reasons. The answer is, I didn't. I don't subscribe to that magazine, and I was nowhere near their house that evening. I was at home with my daughter, who will be happy to confirm that."

"Who else could it have been?" McCord thought out loud. "Pamela Boyd? Aiden Springfield?"

"I can't imagine either of them doing that," Murray said. "Aiden never went anywhere near the house. He told me once he didn't want to get Keira into trouble with her husband, so when he saw her home, he stayed on the main road and watched her go in. And I don't think Pamela ever bought magazines. She despised them. Rubbish in every sense of the word, she always said."

It all sounded very plausible, but McCord deeply distrusted Murray. With the land sale, he had deceived the public and the other members of the group, and McCord didn't believe that the small matter of illegality would have stopped him if indeed he had been unaware of it.

"When did you find out that Lambie's project had fallen through?" McCord asked.

"The day after Keira died," Murray said. "It was all over social media. People were saying that Jordan's project was illegal and that lawsuits would be coming his way unless it was dropped immediately. That was Pamela's doing, of course. She was jumping with joy."

"I bet you weren't," McCord said. "Did you actually get your money from the land sale?"

"Not yet; it was all a bit of a rush. But I do have the paperwork, and I hope that the executor of the will pays me asap. I need it for my daughter's treatment, you know. Otherwise…" His voice trailed off.

McCord felt a show of sympathy was expected of him, but he couldn't bring himself to utter the words.

"Thank you for clearing that up, Mr Murray," he said instead. "Goodbye."

McCord turned to Calderwood. "No joy there," he said. "Have we heard back from the techies about Keira Lambie's phone?"

"Yes, they say the phone was in their house or very near it, and it hadn't been switched off or moved."

"How odd," McCord said. "If it was on, she could have found it by calling it from her husband's phone."

"Unless it was on silent," Calderwood pointed out.

"Still. They lived in a very tidy house, as far as I could see. How could she have lost her phone for more than a day?"

"She could have been on detox," Calderwood said. "Some people do that when they feel that social media is taking over their lives. But then, she would have switched her phone off, wouldn't she?"

McCord shrugged. "We know that she wasn't active on any social media platforms, and she didn't have that many contacts. I can imagine that she wanted to get away from Springfield and his declarations of love, and perhaps from Murray too, but why from Boyd, who was her only close friend?"

"I think we should be concentrating on Upshaw," Calderwood said. "He is still our prime suspect for Keira's murder – or manslaughter at the very least. If we can't nail him for that, then why don't we try to get him for sex offences? If Keira Lambie was only fifteen when Upshaw took up with her, he broke the law."

"I wondered about that myself," McCord said, "but there won't be any proof. Declan Carr is clearly biased as well as an unreliable witness, and Keira's foster parents didn't know what was going on or didn't care; otherwise, they would have done something about it at the time."

Calderwood refreshed the screen on his phone.

"Shouldn't you be getting ready for the wedding?" he asked. "It's one o'clock."

McCord jumped up. "Oh, dammit! My dad and Clare are picking me up at home at quarter to two!"

"I take it you've done your speech?" Calderwood asked.

McCord shrugged with a hangdog expression. "Sort of."

"What do you mean, sort of?"

"I copied one from the Internet."

Calderwood shook his head disapprovingly.

"I know, it's pathetic," McCord said, "but it's better than nothing."

Calderwood opened a drawer in his desk, pulled out an envelope and handed it to McCord. "I prepared this in case you left things to the last minute. You might be able to use it."

"You wrote my speech for me?" McCord asked, a glimmer of hope in his eyes.

Calderwood's expression was difficult to read.

"No, I didn't. Nobody can write your speech for you. But this might help."

McCord tried to hide his disappointment. "Thanks. I just wish this whole bloody wedding was over!"

* * *

"Mum! What the hell is this?!"

Amy stared in horror at the mass of glittering sequins hanging off the dummy in Valerie's boutique. "A mermaid skirt? I'm going to look half human, half sardine! What happened to the fabric you used to measure me?"

Amy's eyes narrowed as a suspicion crept into her head.

"Are you trying to sabotage my date with McCord by any chance? I thought we had this conversation!"

"You said it wasn't a date," Valerie retorted. "You said—"

"Don't change the subject," Amy interrupted. "What made you think I'd put on this monstrosity?"

Valerie was not giving up yet.

"I thought for a wedding you should wear something more glamourous. Something that makes you stand out."

"I'll stand out alright in that. Keith and Clare's guests aren't your upper-class clientele. They're people with modest incomes who will dress up in their finest, and I'm turning up as if I'm a Hollywood star, or rather somebody who would like to be a Hollywood star but isn't."

"But you are a star," Valerie said. "You could do so much better—"

"Better than a detective inspector?" Amy spluttered. "I don't believe I'm hearing this. Have you forgotten where we were before John came on the scene and with his contacts made you an international designer? We shared a tiny flat above your shop on South Bridge and struggled to pay the bills, remember?"

To her surprise, she noticed tears in Valerie's eyes.

"Mum? What *is* the matter with you?" Amy asked, alarmed.

Valerie pulled her daughter into one of her rib-crunching embraces.

"I'm just afraid of losing you," she whispered into Amy's ear. "To a man who doesn't treat you right."

Amy stroked her mother's back. It had taken Valerie two decades to trust a man again after Amy's father had told her to get rid of the baby and sent her on her way. For all this time, Amy had been everything to Valerie until John with his unwavering devotion had coaxed her into a relationship and become a loving stepfather to Amy.

"I won't let any man treat me badly," Amy said. "And you won't lose me, I promise."

Valerie now cried in earnest and squeezed her even harder. Fighting for breath, Amy struggled against the suffocating embrace.

"Ouch! Mum! You've got a nerve warning me off McCord when you're crushing me to death!"

With a croaky laugh, Valerie released her daughter and wiped away the tears with the back of her hand.

"I'm so sorry. What on earth are you going to wear?"

"What I was going to wear in the first place," Amy said. "My tartan skirt is perfect for the ceilidh."

With a sigh, Valerie eyed her latest creation. "Now, what are we going to do with that thing?"

"It'll be great for a fancy-dress party," Amy said with a grin. "I'll go as a mermaid, and then I won't even need a top."

Chapter 27

Dalhousie Castle is a solid red stone pile covered in vine leaves, eight miles south of Edinburgh. At first, McCord had made a face when he was told of the venue which, to him, was an embodiment of the class system that, despite the vigorous efforts of the left, permeates Scottish society to this day. But when he had seen his dad's and Clare's beaming faces, he was glad he had held his tongue.

Due to the hefty price tag, the original plan had been to have only the ceremony and a dinner for the family in the Dungeon Restaurant, but when Keith McCord had seen the dance floor in the Sir Alexander suite, he had, to McCord's dismay, decided on a ceilidh with friends as well. 'What better way to spend your money than on having fun with the people who are important to you,' he had said, squeezing his son's shoulder.

Several taxis were booked for everybody to be taken home afterwards, but McCord had insisted that the newly-weds would stay the night at the place where the long-legged King Edward I and Oliver Cromwell had once lain their royal or rebellious heads; an idea which was received with great enthusiasm by both Keith and Clare, and which also neatly solved the problem of what to give them as a wedding present.

Keith had suggested that he and Clare would give McCord and Amy a lift in his battered Vauxhall Astra, so McCord found himself on the back seat waiting for Amy to come out of her flat.

A lump formed in McCord's throat as he watched her bouncing along the pavement in her skin-tight top and tartan mini skirt.

"Fab," Clare said to Amy with a smile as she slid into the back seat, "it'll be a real Scottish wedding." She pointed to her own, long kilt. "The Hildreths don't have their own tartan, so I went for the McCord one to match Keith and Russell's. You don't think that's a bit too much?"

"No, it's great," Amy said, settling next to McCord.

"I haven't worn my kilt for ages," Keith said. "Thankfully, you can let them out in the waist. I just hope it's not going to be too hot. The bloody socks are itching already."

McCord had anticipated an awkward interrogation of Amy by his father, but his fears proved unfounded. Clare and Amy chatted animatedly about the upcoming ceremony, before Keith regaled them with anecdotes about their relations and friends. He had the women in stitches while McCord was quietly wallowing in his misery about the dreaded speech.

When they entered the grand hall, Keith McCord took a deep breath. "Smell this," he said, squeezing Clare's arm. "Hundreds of years of Scottish history, and we're going to make a little bit of history ourselves."

McCord and Amy shared a little smile, both thinking how infectious happiness can be. When the bride and groom had left to get settled into their room, Amy suggested a walk in the grounds before the other guests arrived.

"Good idea," McCord said, "but first, I'd better have a look at that goddamn speech."

Amy smiled. "Want to do a rehearsal with me? I'm sure we'll find a quiet spot somewhere in the garden."

McCord, in a surge of pride, was about to reject her offer when he realised that it came as a great relief.

"Thanks."

A few hundred yards away from the imposing drive, they came across a grassy area overlooking the valley where a free picnic bench beckoned.

They sat down on the warm, dry wood and simultaneously turned their faces into the golden autumn sun. A long, dark winter lay ahead, and these moments were precious. But McCord soon became restless. He pulled a sheet of paper from his sporran and read out the speech he had downloaded from the Internet.

Amy listened without interrupting, but when McCord had finished, she still did not say anything. McCord lowered the sheet and tried to interpret her guarded expression.

"You don't like it," he said.

Amy forced a smile. "It's okay. There's nothing wrong with it."

"But?"

"It's just… not very authentic."

"I know it's rubbish," McCord said. "My dad will be so disappointed. Hell, I can't do this!"

He flung the sheet into the bin that stood next to the table and buried his face in his hands. Amy tentatively laid her hand on his shoulder.

"Why don't you tell your dad how difficult this was for you? He'll understand."

McCord rubbed his face, embarrassed about his outburst. "We don't talk about… stuff. We simply get on with it."

Amy sighed. "Stop beating yourself up about it. Most people copy their wedding speeches from somewhere, and they are rarely great oratory works. The guests don't listen to them anyway," she fibbed, "especially when they're busy digesting their dinner."

She got up and made to retrieve the paper from the bin, but a couple of angry wasps were buzzing about the lid, and Amy quickly pulled her hand away.

"Leave it," McCord said. "That drivel is not worth getting stung for." Then his face lit up. "Hang on."

He opened the flap of the sporran again and pulled out the small envelope Calderwood had handed to him as he had rushed off to get ready for the wedding.

"Calderwood told me this might help. But if he has played a practical joke on me, I'm going to fake a sudden illness and go straight home."

Amy was incredulous. "Duncan wrote the speech for you, and you haven't even read it?"

"He only gave this to me as I left," McCord said defensively. "I haven't had time."

Amy shook her head. "Most of us are terribly nervous about writing a speech, but sensible people don't leave it to the last minute."

"I didn't!" McCord shouted. "I've tried for the past two weeks to get something together but I'm rubbish at making speeches. I felt it had to be my words for Dad and Clare. But they wouldn't come, so I downloaded a template as backup and kept hoping for a sudden inspiration or–"

"The wedding being cancelled?" Amy could not help laughing. Then, suddenly serious again, she said, "If you want things to happen, you need to do something about it."

He wondered if there was another layer of meaning behind this remark, but his anxiety took over, and he ripped open the envelope. First, he pulled out a blank sheet of paper. His heart sank. Then there was another sheet and a pencil with a rubber tip. McCord unfolded the second one and slowly read the typed-out sentences.

Swallowing hard, he lowered the paper onto the rough surface of the table.

"McCord? Are you okay?" Amy asked, alarmed. She had seen him annoyed, angry even, but never emotional. "I can't believe Duncan did this to you. Just wait till I get hold of him; I'll scratch his bloody eyes out!"

"No, no," McCord said, lovingly patting the sheet of paper. "Calderwood is the best friend one could wish for."

McCord read over Calderwood's notes again and immediately began to scribble. Amy furtively peered over his shoulder, but she could not make out the words, so she pretended to enjoy the scenery, while secretly watching him.

Once, he looked up. "No swear words, right? Even if it's authentic?"

Amy thought about Clare and the prim and proper aunt Keith had told them about.

"Better not," Amy said, growing increasingly concerned. "Maybe I can help?"

He shielded his notes as if they were state secrets.

"No, no, I've got this."

After some rubbing out and more scribbling, he put the pencil down and passed the speech to Amy. She frowned at the first paragraph, but then, as she realised what Calderwood had done, a grin spread across her face.

This was not the reaction McCord had hoped for. "It's still rubbish," he stated hopelessly.

"It's certainly not from some soulless chatbot," Amy said with a strange smile playing around the corners of her mouth.

McCord anxiously turned the pencil between his fingers. "So, you think I should use it?"

"It's… very you," Amy said. "And it's short, which will keep everybody happy no matter what you say. Congratulations, McCord, you've cracked it."

Amongst the relief that flooded McCord, another feeling – unfamiliar and unsettling – tried to assert itself, but he put it down to stage fright and put paper and pencil back into his sporran.

He needed to get rid of some of his nervous energy, so they spent the remaining time before the ceremony wandering around the garden.

McCord pointed out a jay with its colourful wings sailing into a pine, and a great spotted woodpecker whose manic hammering at the bark of an oak tree made Amy laugh.

After a while, they came to a long, low-slung building consisting mainly of large cages. In front of them, a peregrine falcon and a hawk sat perched on wooden poles, enjoying the late afternoon sun, just as Amy and McCord had done. The raptors' jesses had been tied to a leash which in turn was attached to a long, thin chain that lay on the concrete floor. The birds turned their sharp-beaked heads towards the approaching humans and shifted sideways, their talons stretching and contracting with each step.

"Aren't they beautiful?" Amy exclaimed.

McCord looked into the falcon's shiny, nut-brown eyes.

"He's aware of what is happening around him but at the same time he can spot his prey from a mile away; and when he's above it, he dives at over one hundred and twenty miles per hour," McCord said.

"Wow!" Amy exclaimed. "Imagine having tamed them and being able to hold them!"

"I prefer to see them in the wild, free, and hunting for themselves," McCord said.

"I suppose, they have a safer and more comfortable life here," Amy said. "It's a shame, though, that they are tied up. Is that really necessary? Wouldn't they come back of their own accord?"

"They would, because they've learned that there's an easy meal for them here," McCord said. "But if they're tethered, it's easier for the owners to handle them. And to show them off to paying visitors."

Amy had sensed McCord's disapproval.

"Freedom is very important to you, isn't it?" she asked.

"Unlike wild birds, humans are never free," McCord said, "but we all chase the illusion of it."

They moved on and soon forgot about their surroundings, talking about how their upbringing by single parents had shaped them.

"I think we were both very lucky," Amy said, "being brought up by such loving parents, in their different ways; and it's wonderful that both of them have found real happiness later in life."

"I just wish Dad and Clare weren't getting married," McCord said. "They've been perfectly happy until now without all this palaver."

Amy smiled. "You'll enjoy yourself once that speech is out of the way."

"No, I won't," he said. "Afterwards, I'll be mortified about having made a fool of myself."

Amy laughed and squeezed his arm. "You'll be fine. Duncan said you've been a nervous wreck ever since your dad's engagement, but your speech is very good now."

Several taxis were arriving at the entrance of the castle, so they made their way back, each wondering what the evening would bring.

* * *

To McCord's delight, the ceremony itself was brief and carried a message he approved of. The spouse was not to be regarded as property or even as somebody who 'belongs to' their partner, but as a person who needs nurturing and space to grow within the marriage. McCord's thoughts drifted back to Anthony Upshaw and Jordan Lambie, who would both have greatly benefitted from this advice.

"It takes faith and courage," the officiant was saying, "to allow the other person the freedom to leave, and trust that they are going to stay with you from choice."

In a flash of inspiration, McCord understood what had happened to the Lambies' marriage. Beth Lambie had said that Jordan loved Keira deeply, but feeling abandoned by his dead mother, unloving father and calculating first wife, he hadn't had the courage to allow Keira her freedom, especially when she became friendly with people who were no friends of his. In the end, he even took her phone away and imprisoned her until he realised the madness of his actions and took her to The Balerno Inn where he begged her to forgive him and to give their marriage another chance.

"The rings?" The stern voice of the officiant catapulted him back into the present, and blushing to the roots of his dark hair, he fumbled in his pocket for the rings. Thank God, they were there. He handed the larger one to his dad, who shot him a quizzical look, and the smaller one to Clare, who smiled indulgently.

McCord felt Amy's eyes on him and realised to his surprise that he couldn't wait to tell her what he had figured out.

After the ceremony had concluded without any further embarrassment, the happy couple and the guests mingled, sipping prosecco.

Clare's grown-up children, who had met McCord before, cheerfully asked him about crime and birds, which they knew he found an easy topic for conversation. Despite their best efforts, however, McCord had withdrawn into a world of his own, so they turned to Amy, gently interrogating the journalist who had helped solve so many crimes and, belying McCord's assurances to the contrary, looked very much to be his girlfriend.

Eventually, McCord and Amy managed to extricate themselves from the relatives and friends, and stepped outside into a plush corridor with dark-wood panelling and carpets so thick that both their steps and their voices were muffled.

Listening carefully to McCord's account of that fateful evening, Amy nodded. "It makes sense," she said. "Keira assures Jordan that she has been loyal and faithful to him, and all is well until he finds the magazine on the doormat. All his dreams come tumbling down, and reading the article, he believes that it was Keira who tipped Martin off about his illegal land sale, and that she betrayed him after all."

"We know from Listerman's account of Lambie attacking the bullies at their school that he had a temper on him," McCord spun the story further. "He sees red and goes for Keira, who runs away from him, falls and hits her head."

"He is still mad at her and not prepared to go to prison for the rest of his life because of a woman who betrayed him," Amy picked up the thread. "He stages a break-in. Upshaw was the ideal candidate; he deserved to be in prison anyway. And Jordan burnt the magazine because that might have told us what this had been all about."

They smiled at each other, pleased to have put together one part of the puzzle.

"This is such fun," Amy said. "I love… solving crimes with you… and the team."

McCord swallowed, wondering whether 'me, too' would sound corny and insincere. "We've still got Jordan Lambie's murderer on the loose, though," he said instead.

It was almost an hour until dinner. They had no inclination to make any more small talk, so Amy fetched her jacket from the hallstand, and they sneaked out again.

Amy kept speculating about Jordan Lambie's murder, which was fruitless but at least distracted McCord from his increasing stage fright.

As they walked in the shade of a huge, old beech tree where it was almost dark, Amy stumbled over the ruts on the path and grabbed McCord's arm. His muscles tensing, he steadied her without a word.

"I can't see a thing," Amy said, hanging on, but even when they stepped out of the shadows, she left her arm resting on his, just in case, and they fell into a comfortable rhythm again.

Soon, they heard loud voices wafting over from the courtyard calling people inside.

"I think it's time for dinner," Amy said.

As they approached the entrance, where the other guests were gathering, Amy disengaged herself from McCord. She didn't want to make him more uncomfortable than he was already.

He turned to her. "I'll take your coat," he said, slipping it off her shoulder and hanging it on the stand next to his.

Then he offered her his arm.

"Shall we go in?"

Chapter 28

One advantage of people getting married later in life is that there tend to be fewer speeches. First, it was Keith McCord's turn to thank the guests for coming. His account of how he and Clare had met was very amusing. She had engraved his bowling trophy for him and phoned to check the spelling of his name. After a brief conversation, Keith had asked Clare if she wanted to go to the cinema with him, and the rest was, as they say, history.

"After being on my own for so long," Keith said, looking in McCord's direction, "it took a lot of courage to ask a woman out, but it was the best thing I have ever done in my life. Cheers!"

His speech went down well, as did the French wine, and by the time the dessert had been consumed, the wedding party was rather merry.

McCord threw a glance at Amy, who nodded encouragingly. He rose and pinged on his glass a couple of times.

"Dad, Clare, ladies and gentlemen," he began.

His airways had suddenly constricted, so he took a deep breath, cleared his throat and took the plunge.

"In the run-up to this occasion, while I was trying to write this speech, I strongly felt that marriage as an institution should be abolished. Let's be honest, what's the point? Why the hell do people get married? The best people are living in sin, like my DS, for example, who, incidentally, helped me write this speech. There's really no need anymore these days to sign your life over to one single person, is there?"

A ripple of uncertain laughter went through the party, and by now he had everybody's attention as people wanted to see if this was going to go from bad to worse.

"What I've learned from my current case," he ploughed on, "is that marriage is a minefield. And not only that; if we believe that it is a celebration of love that lasts for the rest of people's lives, it inevitably ends with at least one of the participants dead."

Keith burst out laughing and Clare pressed a linen napkin to her mouth, but most of the guests were exchanging bewildered looks.

"Which I hope is a long way away for both of you," McCord added hastily as he had a notion that not everybody here shared his sense of humour.

He looked beseechingly at Amy, who smiled and mouthed 'go on'.

"The first time I realised that something weird was happening to my dad was when he began to exhibit very strange behaviour." He looked at Keith, who grinned. "It was a relief to find out that it was not a mental illness as such, but that he was in love."

A wave of mirth went through the room, and thus encouraged, McCord continued with more confidence.

"Before I met her, I was quite apprehensive about this new woman coming into our lives. It had always been me and Dad. Just us. Our curry night was the highlight of my week and, until then, it had been sacrosanct. I was afraid that all that would change. But to my great relief, Clare wasn't the stereotypical evil stepmother, but actually quite nice."

"Well, thank you very much," Clare interjected with a laugh.

"And soon I realised," McCord plodded on desperately, "that these two are perfect for each other. They fit together like two pieces of a jigsaw. My dad loves

Clare, and she loves him. I love my dad, so I'm happy for them both. End of story. What is there to speechify about? So, a toast to the best dad anybody could wish for and his lovely wife. Keith and Clare!"

"Keith and Clare!" echoed cheerfully around the room.

As McCord sat down, wiping his brow, Keith patted his son's shoulder with a grin.

"Great speech, son. Short, to the point and funny. I told you it would be a piece of cake!"

* * *

Keith and Clare's budget had not stretched to a live band, but one of her children had put together a playlist and talked the guests through the dance steps.

Keen to avoid any further unnecessary embarrassment, McCord had used videos on YouTube to prime himself for the usual ceilidh favourites. He even got through the eightsome reel without treading on too many toes and was gratified to see Amy's flushed, happy face as she swirled, stomped and clapped to the relentless fiddling. Before it was time for the strains of Strip the Willow, he quickly went off to get them drinks, but upon his return, he found that one of his dad's inebriated bowling companions had exploited the opportunity, unceremoniously grabbed Amy's arm and dragged her onto the dance floor. With a regretful glance towards McCord, Amy followed the man, who had the triumphant air of a successful trophy hunter.

McCord, in turn, was claimed by one of Clare's friends. Whether her heaving bosom was caused by the previous exercise or the excitement of having procured a dance with a handsome younger man, McCord was not sure, but he fervently hoped it was the former.

Amy and her partner were two places up from McCord, and he watched with growing fury and concern the way the drunken oaf hurled Amy about. She struggled to keep her bare feet on the floor. When it was McCord's two-second turn to swing with Amy, she rolled her eyes, and he mouthed a silent 'sorry' before she was flung about again.

The show-off had not considered his own precarious situation, however, and when his sweaty fingers lost their grip on Amy's hand, he careered into the line of dancers and, with a yelp of pain, collapsed on the floor.

He was immediately surrounded by his concerned fellow dancers. Both alcohol and pain made him slur his speech as he swore profusely and tried to clutch his expanding ankle, which, due to his protruding belly, he was unable to do.

"So sore," he mumbled. "I… need… i…bu…profen."

McCord, who had been watching the moron's predicament with secret satisfaction, froze. All the puzzle pieces that had been swirling around in his brain suddenly fell into place. He nudged Amy, who was only half-heartedly commiserating with her ill-fated dance partner, and he motioned her to follow him outside.

"I've figured it out," he said, his eyes shining.

Amy recognised the look and barely contained her excitement. "What? Tell me!"

"That's what Keira Lambie tried to say before she died," McCord said. "Not 'aye but proven' but 'ibuprofen'. It was her who switched Jordan Lambie's meds."

Amy slapped her forehead.

"Of course! When he took her phone away and imprisoned her in the house, she was trapped, but she was determined not to let herself become a victim again." Her enthusiasm gave way to a frown. "But why would she want to save him when he had just attacked her?"

"Because she realised that it was not his fault," McCord said. "It was somebody else who manipulated them both into thinking the worst of each other."

Amy stared at him. "Who? How?"

"After Jordan Lambie had imprisoned Keira, he came to his senses," McCord went on. "He took her out to dinner, asked her forgiveness and begged her to give their marriage another chance. She probably remembered how happy they had been in the early days and agreed. All was well, but when they came home, he found *Forth Write* on the mat and saw Martin's article. Believing that Keira had betrayed him, he went for her, so she had had no time to switch the meds back as she had intended. That is what she was desperate to tell the ambulance driver. In the end, she tried to save him, but it was too late." He shook his head. "What a terrible, terrible tragedy: they killed each other by mistake."

"Still, it was all his fault!" Amy said. "There's no excuse for imprisoning and attacking your wife!"

"Of course not," McCord said. "But he saw himself as her protector; for him, it was the two of them against the world. And when she began to reject his overbearing protection, he was afraid of losing her to another man or even to a political cause."

Amy nodded thoughtfully.

"He tried to hold on to her at any cost, and ironically, that's what drove her away," she said. "But you think they were being manipulated; if that's the case, by whom?"

"Who kept on and on at Keira to leave her husband, suggesting to her that he was dangerous? Who dropped off the magazine that pushed Jordan Lambie over the edge? I thought that the magazine was supposed to warn him, but I was wrong. It was meant to make Jordan angry and suspicious. Perhaps she even hoped he would attack Keira so that she could keep her position of power in the group."

Amy's eyes widened. "Pamela Boyd?" she whispered.

"Yes," McCord said. "She told me that Keira's last message to her was about swapping computer files, which Keira hadn't managed to do. That was a lie. According to Donald Murray, Keira was great with IT. I think that Boyd suggested to Keira that she could free herself from her evil husband by swapping his meds, which would very conveniently get rid of her political arch enemy, too. At that point, Keira answered that she couldn't do it; she still loved her husband. But when he took her phone away and locked her up, she thought she was dealing with another Upshaw, and something inside her snapped."

Amy nodded. "Some stalking victims think about suicide, but Keira decided to fight. In her mind, it was the only way she could be free again."

"So," McCord spun the story on, "after Jordan Lambie had killed Keira, he was left thinking that she had betrayed and ruined him, until her funeral, when Aiden Springfield decided to give him a piece of his mind. I'm sure our dreamy poet has no idea that he lit the fuse on a cache of explosives then. Jordan Lambie realised that Boyd had not only destroyed his project by putting pressure on Listerman, but, even worse, she had poisoned Keira's mind against him and his against her."

"No wonder Jordan lost it," Amy said. "Imagine killing the woman you love and then finding out that you've been played."

McCord gave her a look that was difficult to read. "I can't imagine that," he said. "But, I suppose, we never know what we are capable of. Anyway, Lambie comes across Boyd outside. The kind of person she was, she probably goaded him, as well, and bang, he takes revenge. I wonder if he had realised that he was dying."

Amy knew what McCord was thinking. "You did everything you could to save him. Without his medication, he had no chance. And perhaps he was resigned to it. Having lost Keira and his dream, he had nothing to live for, did he?"

"I suppose not," McCord said.

They fell silent as Keith and some of his friends were walking past them, helping the unfortunate dancer to the door where a taxi was waiting to take him home.

"Trust the bloody job," McCord said, watching his dad with fondness, "to ruin even his wedding."

"Why?" Amy said. "You're not thinking of going to St Leonard's now, are you?"

"I'm running a murder investigation," McCord said.

Amy held up her hands. "And what are you going to achieve there? Tonight? Both killers are dead. Justice, in a bizarre fashion, has been done."

"Not quite," McCord said. "Upshaw is still out there. And when you think about it, this whole mess is his fault. If he hadn't hounded Keira out of Glasgow in the first place, none of this would have happened. But I can't see a way to get a conviction for him, I really can't."

Amy laid her hand on his arm. "Let's leave it until tomorrow. The ceilidh is finished, by the sounds of it, but there's still the disco to come."

She laughed at his horrified expression. "It's much easier than country dancing. You don't have to do anything but to go with the rhythm, see?" She swayed her hips in time to the ABBA tune that was bursting from the loudspeakers. "Come on, I won't take 'no' for an answer."

McCord closed his eyes. "If you want to be embarrassed by me, fine. But I need a drink first."

As they approached the bar, Amy clapped her hands like an excited child.

"I know," she said. "What you need is a bit of fizz. That really loosened you up the last time."

The bartender had heard her and passed her the cocktail menu before she had a chance to ask.

"May I recommend our special – The Dalhousie Sundowner? Prosecco, gin and cranberry juice."

"Sounds great," Amy said. "Two of those, please."

McCord groaned.

"God, no. The last time you chose my drinks, I ended up on your sofa."

A mischievous smile played around Amy's lips. "Don't worry, that's not going to happen again."

Chapter 29

The following day, McCord did not turn up at St Leonard's until the afternoon, a fact that was commented on unfavourably by Gilchrist whose reading of the tabloids had brought him one step closer to a recurrence of his stomach ulcer.

It took McCord a while to unravel the story into easily comprehensible strands. When he had finished, the superintendent expressed his satisfaction that all current cases were now closed.

"Although," he added, "the last two murders could have been prevented if you had been more switched on and interpreted Keira Lambie's last words correctly in the first place. And regarding the fact that a prominent activist was killed right under your nose, well, let's say no more about that."

Normally, McCord would have been contemplating the method he would employ when he finally snapped and killed his boss – blunt force trauma, definitely – but today, he felt strangely invincible.

"Miss Thornton's article will be out soon, and no doubt, she'll get our side of the story across," he said.

Gilchrist's face brightened up. "That's excellent news." He laughed at his own pun. "I don't know what we'd do without her. She always makes you out to be the hero, though; no idea how she manages that." Gilchrist seemed genuinely puzzled. "She does have a bee in her bonnet about stalkers, as well. Her last article was rather uncomplimentary about Police Scotland, but at least it's got nothing to do with my department. We've done our job, and if the odd stalker cannot be prosecuted, it's not the problem of Edinburgh CID."

For the first time in his life, McCord felt simply unable to be annoyed with Gilchrist. He even agreed with him on the last point. But he could hear Amy's furious response in his head and felt compelled to give her a voice.

"Everybody should make it their problem," McCord said. "Upshaw ruined Keira Lambie's life, and he is going to get away with it unless something is done about him. Can't we at least issue a formal warning?"

Gilchrist shook his head.

"No. You've just told me yourself that we have nothing on Upshaw. Keira Lambie withdrew her original complaint against him, and his mother won't allow us to harass him on spurious grounds. Hopefully now that his target is dead, he'll stop."

But the little Amy in his head was not willing to let this go.

"And what if he chooses another woman to torment?" McCord asked Gilchrist.

The superintendent shrugged. "At least we won't be involved unless he kills somebody on our patch. Which seems highly unlikely," he added, seeing McCord's expression. "No, all three cases closed and thank God for that."

* * *

Back in his office, even the thought of Upshaw getting away scot-free barely dented McCord's new-found serenity. Calderwood, being the gentleman he was, hadn't asked him why he had come into work so late today, but McCord deduced from his partner's knowing smile that he had guessed the reason correctly.

"Amy told me to phone her as soon as the meeting with Gilchrist is over," McCord said. "She won't be happy."

"She must know that there's a limit to what we can do," Calderwood said. "Unfortunately, some just get away."

"Wise words, Calderwood, which will do nothing to appease her."

With a sigh, he pressed the green button.

"Hi," Amy said with a seductiveness in her voice that made Calderwood grin.

McCord noisily cleared his throat.

"Hi," he said in a business-like tone. "You're on loudspeaker. It's a 'no' from Gilchrist. And Calderwood, who is sitting here with me," he added pointedly, "agrees. We've come to the end of the road with Upshaw. I'm sorry," he added, bracing himself for a dose of her wrath.

Amy, however, seemed quite unperturbed.

"That was to be expected, I suppose. Thanks for trying, anyway. Shall we meet up later tonight?"

"Sure," McCord said. "I'll give you a call when I'm finished here."

"Great. Can't wait. Bye!"

The line went dead.

"That was weird," McCord said.

With a little laugh, Calderwood pointed out that this was the kind of conversation normal couples had.

But McCord sat silently, a deep frown on his forehead.

Calderwood watched him, half amused, half concerned.

"The start of a relationship can feel a little overwhelming, but isn't it wonder–"

"No, no, no," McCord said, shaking his head. "That was weird."

* * *

When Patricia Upshaw opened the stained-glass door of her Victorian villa after three rings of the melodious bell, she took in Amy's elegant outfit and confident bearing and decided not to slam the door in her face. At least not immediately.

"Yes?" she asked with a forced smile.

"I'm Amy Thornton from *Forth Write* magazine. May I come in?"

For a moment, Amy feared that Patricia Upshaw might recognise her voice, or her nose, from their previous encounter at Tunnock's car park.

"I'm afraid not," Patricia Upshaw said with insincere regret. "I don't give interviews to the press. I'm sorry," she added, no doubt thinking it wise not to antagonise a journalist unnecessarily.

"I don't want an interview," Amy said quickly before Patricia Upshaw could close the door. "I've come to warn you of an imminent danger to you and your son."

"What danger?" Patricia Upshaw asked, disbelief and curiosity vying for supremacy in her features.

"Perhaps we'd better discuss this inside?"

Amy pointed to the open windows next door and moved towards the threshold. "I'm sure your neighbours would love to know–"

"Come in," Patricia Upshaw said and hastily closed the door behind Amy. "The living room is through there."

They entered a spacious, sunlit room with a large bay window looking out over a neat front garden. The furnishings were exquisite without being ostentatious and would have served well for an edition of *House Beautiful*, especially as the room was devoid of any personal touch, let alone clutter.

Amy saw Patricia Upshaw dither over whether to offer a refreshment, which would have necessitated leaving her uninvited guest without supervision, or not to offer anything, which would be rude. Amy did nothing to help; with an expectant smile, she sat on the discreetly patterned tartan sofa and watched her host trying to get the measure of her.

Patricia Upshaw sat down in an armchair opposite Amy, having decided not to take the risk of a reporter snooping around her house. "What did you mean by danger?" she asked.

"The danger of negative press coverage of your son's, shall we say, eagerness to be close to women who would rather be left alone," Amy said.

"There is no danger," Mrs Upshaw said coldly. "He hasn't broken any laws, and if anybody even suggests that he has, I'm going to sue them." She rose. "Thank you for your concern, but there was no need. Goodbye."

Amy, her smile fading, didn't move an inch.

"We both know that your son stalked Keira McInver, as she was then, entered her home without permission and raped her when she lived in Glasgow; and that you threatened and bribed the victim to make the complaint go away."

Patricia Upshaw opened her mouth to protest, but Amy silenced her with a wave of the hand. "I have a copy of the bank statements to prove it. I have also spoken to Keira's former flatmate who found Keira after your son's attack. She gave a very vivid description of the state Keira was in. In fact, I have several people who would be very happy to be quoted in our paper, with the usual caveats, of course." She gave a little laugh. "We have a saying at *Forth Write* magazine: one 'alleged' a day keeps the libel away – would you mind sitting down? My neck is beginning to hurt."

Patricia Upshaw, however, remained standing, towering over Amy and watching her with narrowed eyes. Amy leaned back and crossed her legs as if they were discussing the weather.

"As you wish," Amy said. "Next week, I'll be starting an Internet campaign against stalking which will run until the cases in Scotland are down by fifty per cent. That should take a few years at least, judging by the way the police and the legal profession" – she regarded Patricia

Upshaw with a meaningful tilt of the head – "have been handling those cases. And every single week I'm going to mention your son's alleged crimes and your alleged complicity."

"How dare you?" Patricia Upshaw snapped. "You can't destroy our reputation like that!"

"That's the only thing that you've ever cared about," Amy said, "your reputation. And I can and will destroy it. Social media is a terrible thing, isn't it? It can spread the word so quickly and so widely… There's an ever-growing number of people who feel very strongly about misogyny and violence towards women, and once a post has been shared a few thousand times… you can't prosecute them all, you know."

A sneer of disgust distorted Patricia Upshaw's mouth.

"Enough said. How much do you want?"

Amy smiled contemptuously.

"I don't want your money. I consider it my citizen's duty to publicise your son's crimes and the fact that you, a member of the legal profession, helped him evade justice. Unless…"

"Unless?" If Patricia Upshaw felt any hope or fear, she did not show it.

"Unless you make Anthony confess to stalking and raping Keira."

Patricia Upshaw guffawed.

"Don't be ridiculous. That's never going to happen!"

She moved forward, a cornered animal ready to attack.

Amy's fingers slipped around the self-defence spray concealed in her handbag. She wished now she had confided in McCord or Calderwood, but she hadn't wanted to drag either of them into this murky business that she strongly suspected to be illegal. And anyway, both of them would have prevented her from doing what had to be done.

Seeing the red-and-black spray can pointed at her face, Patricia Upshaw quickly regained her self-control.

"Please sit down, Mrs Upshaw," Amy said. "I have left instructions with my lawyer, so attacking me would only make matters worse for you – and for Anthony."

Once Mrs Upshaw had obeyed, Amy, still clasping the spray, lowered her hand into her lap.

"Now," Amy continued, "if Anthony comes forward voluntarily, his sentence will be reduced by, let's say, half. With good conduct, the time he needs to serve will no doubt be halved again. He'll be out in no time. Nowhere near enough punishment for him, but at least something."

"Don't be ridiculous!" Patricia Upshaw repeated, but the denial had lost some of its vigour.

Amy ignored the refusal. "After serving his sentence, Anthony will be going into a clinic for therapy. Considering the state of mental healthcare in this country, you will have to go private, I'm afraid, but having been a lawyer, I'm sure you can afford it."

She made a show of evaluating the expensive interior before fixing her gaze again on Patricia Upshaw.

"And if I ever," Amy said very slowly, "hear a hint of a rumour of a further complaint against Anthony on my extensive social network, I will make sure that his sentence will be far less lenient next time."

"There is no need for all this." Patricia Upshaw's trembling hands belied the confidence in her voice. "There won't be any future complaint against him. I'll make sure of that. It was just that one girl–"

"Who is now dead," Amy finished the sentence with a steely voice.

"Which had nothing to do with Anthony or me!"

Amy laughed incredulously.

"It had everything to do with you and him," she said. "Keira would never have left Glasgow if it hadn't been for you and your son. If he hadn't frightened her out of her wits, this whole tragedy would not have happened. And now you have a choice. Do you understand?"

The fight had not yet left Patricia Upshaw.

"Oh, yes! I understand perfectly well!" She leant forward in her seat, her spittle spraying Amy's face, who recoiled in disgust. "This is not only blackmail; you are also threatening me with an offensive weapon. These so-called self-defence sprays are still illegal in the UK, no matter what the sellers claim. I'm going to speak to Superintendent Gilchrist, and he will put an end to this outrage!"

"Please yourself," Amy said with a shrug. "I know Superintendent Gilchrist personally through my long-standing association with Edinburgh CID, and he greatly values my contributions; my boss, John Campbell, plays golf with the assistant chief constable, who is a close family friend; and just in case you're thinking of taking your displeasure out on Detective Inspector McCord, he won a bravery award earlier this year, and the assistant chief constable thinks very highly of him."

Amy paused to let this sink in. "But do go ahead; a lawyer trying to prevent justice from being done will add some spice to a story that might otherwise become a little dull over time."

Amy's eyes locked with Patricia Upshaw's as she rose with a mirthless smile and put the spray back into her handbag. "I suggest you act quickly. On Saturday, my story about the Lambie and Boyd murder cases will come out. Whether you and your son feature in it or not, depends entirely on Anthony's actions."

She made her way to the door but turned on the threshold.

"Oh, and when the time comes for your son to be released, I expect copies of the therapy bills and the final report to be sent to my address at *Forth Write* magazine. Goodbye, Mrs Upshaw. Thanks for the lovely chat. I'll see myself out."

In the corridor, Amy kept looking backwards in case Patricia Upshaw decided to come after her and swing a golf club at her head, but her host was still sitting upright in her armchair, staring into space.

Amy stepped out into the foggy afternoon as the heavy oak door clunked shut. Only now that the deed was done did her knees begin to tremble. She closed her eyes and inhaled the sweet, earthy fragrance of the autumn leaves littering the pavement. After a few deep breaths, her legs felt steady enough to carry her along the quiet residential street towards her mother's MG. Playing the conversation with Mrs Upshaw over in her head and telling herself that she had achieved all she could, she didn't notice the car speeding towards her from behind, until it came to a screeching halt right next to her. Yelping with fear, Amy stumbled sideways into a privet hedge rising above a low stone wall.

Muttering curses, she straightened up again only to see McCord jump out of his Juke, a mixture of anger, concern and relief on his face. "Are you alright?"

Furious, Amy brushed overripe berries and damp leaves off her skirt and the delicately stitched bolero that Valerie had made for her.

"I was until you gave me the fright of my life. What are you doing here?" She stemmed her fists on her hips. "Have you been spying on me?"

"Just making sure you didn't get hit over the head with a leather briefcase," McCord retorted. "I knew you wouldn't let the matter with Upshaw rest. If I'd been two minutes earlier, I would have broken the door down."

"Ooh," Amy cooed, pretending to wobble and faint, "and I'm supposed to sink into my hero's arms now, am I?"

"That was the general idea," McCord said. "But, of course, I got it wrong again."

"Spectacularly," Amy said, inspecting the ladders in her tights. "Anyway, how did you know I'd be here? I didn't tell a soul!"

McCord grinned.

"Sutton needed less than a minute to locate your phone on the M8 moving towards Glasgow."

"I'm going to have a word with her about privacy laws," Amy said. "You almost ruined the whole plan."

"And what plan is that exactly?" he asked. "I have a terrible suspicion that it involves some degree of criminality."

"Then you're better off not knowing," Amy said. "But I believe justice will be done. You'll simply have to wait and see."

She smiled triumphantly, and he knew she enjoyed this game far too much to give in and satisfy his curiosity.

He put on a grave face. "May I point out that it is illegal to withhold evidence from the police – which is me, in case you have forgotten. I'm afraid it is my professional duty to subject you to the most thorough interrogation."

With a theatrical sigh Amy tilted her head. "I suppose you must… but surely not here in full view of the public. My place?"

"You'll be plying me with mind-bending cocktails again," McCord said in mock-complaint. "And you know where that'll end."

Pretending to be chastened, Amy hung her head.

McCord's face was stern, but there was a twinkle in his eye.

"So, the answer is yes. Definitely your place."

List of characters

Police

Detective Inspector Russell McCord
Detective Sergeant Duncan Calderwood
Superintendent Arthur Gilchrist
Dr Cyril Crane – pathologist
Detective Constable Heather "The Hacker" Sutton
PC Surina Dharwan – DS Calderwood's fiancée
PC Mike Turner
PC Jim Easton
PC Douglas Reid
Fred Foster – forensic lab assistant

Amy Thornton's circle

Amy Thornton – journalist with Forth Write magazine
Simone Fleming – Amy's undercover name
Martin Eden – subeditor of Forth Write magazine
John Campbell – owner of Forth Write magazine
Valerie Thornton – Amy's mother and partner of John Campbell

Others

Keith McCord – father of DI Russell McCord

Clare Hildreth – Keith's fiancée

Jordan Lambie – solar energy developer

Keira Lambie, née McInver – his current wife

Beth Lambie – Jordan Lambie's sister

Janine – Beth Lambie's secretary

Melissa Lambie – Jordan Lambie's first wife

Pamela Boyd – leader of the environmental group The Green Fist

Donald Murray – founder and previous leader of the group

Aiden Springfield – member of The Green Fist

Anthony Upshaw – ex-boyfriend of Keira Lambie

Patricia Upshaw – his mother, a defence lawyer

Louise Braithwaite – Anthony Upshaw's former girlfriend

Rev. Matthew – minister of St Andrews East Parish Church

Jackie Reeves – waitress at The Balerno Inn

Sean Listerman – butcher; old school friend of Jordan Lambie

Declan Carr – childhood friend of Keira Lambie

Alistair Nesbitt – crematorium officer

If you enjoyed this book, please let others know by leaving a quick review on Amazon. Also, if you spot anything untoward in the paperback, get in touch. We strive for the best quality and appreciate reader feedback.

editor@thebookfolks.com

Also in this series

NEAR MISS (book 1)

After being nearly hit by a car, fashion journalist Amy
Thornton decides to visit the driver, who ends up in hospital
after evading her. Curious about this strange man she
becomes convinced she's unveiled a murder plot. But it won't
be so easy to persuade Scottish detective DI Russell McCord.

HIGH HAND (book 2)

When a man is killed after a shooting party on a Scottish
country estate, DI McCord gets nowhere interviewing the
arrogant landowners. He'll have to rely on information passed
on by journalist Amy Thornton, who is more accustomed to
high society. But will his class resentment colour his
judgement when it comes to putting the murderer behind
bars?

LAST TRAIN FOR MURDER (book 3)

An investigative journalist who made a career out of sticking it to the man dies on a train to Edinburgh, having been poisoned. DI Russell McCord struggles in the investigation after getting banned from contacting helpful but self-serving reporter Amy Thornton. But the latter is ready to go in, all guns blazing. After the smoke has cleared, what will remain standing?

SHIFTING ICE (book 4)

After a jewellery thief meets a bitter end, DI McCord tries to make sense of his dying words. Are they a clue to his killer? He'll find out. Meanwhile journalist Amy Thornton is forbidden from taking on dangerous investigations, and sent on a fool's errand. Hmmm. She'll wiggle out of just about anything. Except perhaps the place she might hold in the cop's heart.

BRIGHT SPARKS (book 5)

The death of a local businesswoman in a house fire has grumpy detective Russell McCord running around in circles looking for the culprit. Sassy journalist Amy Thornton has some ideas of her own. But when the smoke has cleared, can the two crime-solvers put their differences aside and their heads together to work out the truth?

FICKLE FORTUNES (book 6)

When a woman suffers a fatal fall from an iconic beauty spot
in Edinburgh, DI Russell McCord believes her husband
pushed her over the edge. Amateur sleuth Amy Thornton is
not so sure, and digs around places McCord neglects. It turns
out that the victim's life was full of secrets, and one of them
is key to solving her murder.

Other titles of interest

MURDER IN THE NEW FOREST
by Carol Cole

When a woman's body is found on the ground next to her
horse, it seems an unfortunate accident had occurred.
However, DI Callum MacLean, newly arrived in the
picturesque New Forest from Glasgow, suspects differently.
But hunting a killer in this close-knit community, suspicious
of outsiders, will be tough. Especially when not everyone in
his team is on side.

THAT CARE FORGOT
by James Warren

Junior attorney Rebecca Holt isn't too happy when given the pro bono case of a convicted murderer. Yet Nick Malone isn't really interested in his parole hearing, rather he is obsessed with a serial killer who terrorized New Orleans in the 1990s. When Malone reveals his secrets, Rebecca is faced with a life-changing decision.

www.ingramcontent.com/pod-product-compliance
Lightning Source LLC
Chambersburg PA
CBHW030934210726
48290CB00007B/2181